Our Fated Love

Our Fated Love

Our Fated Love

Elizabeth Ptack

Cover design by Sofia Badolato
Cover art by Hannah Bloom

First paperback edition March 2024

ISBN 978-1-7383207-0-7 (paperback)
ISBN 978-1-7383207-1-4 (eBook)
ISBN 978-1-7383207-2-1 (hardcover)

Contact the author at info@ourfatedlove.com

For

All the girls who were never the first

choice.

Our Fated Love

Chapter 1

Kayleigh

The sound of my phone awakens me out of nowhere and I swear I'm going to kill my best friend. Every morning, since we were freshmen, Sadie had to be the first person to call me. To make matters worse, she decided to give herself the most ear-piercing ringtone anyone could imagine. I can feel my ears bleeding by the time I decline Sadie's phone call.

Once I'm up and out of bed, I throw my clothes on relatively quickly. So, I crawl back into the comfort of my bed and try to close my eyes. Not even seconds later, Sadie somehow sensed me dozing off because she comes bursting into my room with enough energy for the both of us.

"I cannot believe you declined my call." She lies down next to me on my bed. "Like seriously, you could've at least answered me. 'Hey, best friend in the entire world?' Or 'how's it going, Sadie.' I expect a lot more from you."

"Go away Sades, I just want to sleep," my voice is muffled under my covers. She springs up from my bed and latches onto the covers that are covering my face.

"Sleep? No way am I letting you sleep in on our first day of Senior year! Come on Kay, let's get you out of bed." She is practically jumping up and down around my room until my feet hit the ground beside my bed.

I do not understand how someone can have so much energy in the morning. Her voice is just beaming with excitement.

When I stand up and expose my outfit for the day, a shriek leaves Sadie's mouth.

"Please tell me that's not what you're wearing today."

Sadie is super into all that fashion stuff.

"What?"

Over the years she has made it very clear that she thinks my style could improve.

One morning I even woke up to her sorting my clothes into three piles.

- Love it!

- Hate it, and

- OMG HELL HAS FROZEN OVER

Have I mentioned she's a tad over dramatic?

Most of my clothes were in the "OMG HELL HAS FROZEN OVER" pile, but I didn't care. I spent the rest of the day putting everything back, even though Sadie strongly suggested I shouldn't. And by strongly suggested, I mean she stormed out of my house and went shopping because, and I quote:

"I already feel my fashion sense leaving me."

I truly do love that girl, but sometimes she is just too much. I've come to the point where I expect to hear at least one comment a day about my style, but I haven't heard it yet so maybe….

"Ok, we got to do something about your style. I just can't be seen with someone who always wears the same thing."

Right on cue.

I look down at my old rag-like shirt that my dad gave me a few years back. It is oversized and has a few holes around the collar. He got it from a concert back in the 80s. It's where he and my mom first fell in love. Their love story is still heartwarming, but it is not like they had a choice; everyone is destined to be with their soulmate. Just thinking about it makes my eyes roll to the back of my head.

The entire concept of everyone being born with one soulmate is the most fucked up thing in the world. Who's to say who someone should fall in love with? Why do we even need a soulmate to make ourselves happy? Are people so self-conscious that they need to be told how much they are loved every second of the day? Or how pretty they are? Seriously, grow the fuck up. I shouldn't need a man in my life, I don't want to worry about someone else's feelings! I can barely handle my own.

By the way that Sadie is glaring at me right now, I can tell that I've worked myself up over this whole soulmate thing. She kinda looks at me as if I was just possessed by a demon ghost. So, I quickly snap out of my trance.

"Well, I happen to really like this shirt.," I say with my proudest voice.

"Yeah, well that makes one of us," replies Sadie.

She is already rummaging through my closet for something else I could wear today. If I wasn't already clear enough, Sades and I have been best friends since before we were even born. She's the sister I've always wanted. Well except Stella, she's my actual baby sister. She's in her preteen years now, and I don't think I have ever met more of a drama queen. Don't get me wrong, I love Stella with all my heart, but holy shit, little sisters can be so annoying.

She is always asking for something, or just takes things out of my room, she figures that anything that's mine is also hers. I have found many of my vinyl's, and jewelry just lying on the floor in her room.

Before I let Sadie dress me up, I make my way to my computer. Most people need their coffee in the morning. I NEED MY MUSIC. I made this awesome playlist that everyone loves, and by everyone, I mean my four best friends. It has every one of my favourite artists ranging from The Rolling Stones to Taylor Swift. I'm mostly into bands or groups but who can ever say no to Taylor?

Now that I'm somewhat awake, I finish getting ready for my last first day of school. It's Senior Year, and I cannot wait for it to be over! This is the year that we age out of finding our soulmates. If people don't find their soulmate by the time of the deadline, they get sent to the Bunker. Everyone is terrified of that place. I don't blame them for being scared, because once you go to the Bunker you never come out. No one truly knows what happens behind those walls.

I walk over to Sadie who is still looking at herself in my vanity mirror. I'm not entirely sure how she can even see her full outfit. I've decorated the mirror over the years with many drawings. But I guess that girl can make anything work. I hate to admit these things, but her outfit is adorable, it screams Sadie. It's this white tennis skirt that barely reaches her knees, with a white collared shirt, that's covered up with her boyfriend's oversized crewneck. The best thing about her outfit though are her shoes. I bought her these plain white tennis shoes that she begged me for, but I added a few of my own details. I painted these monarch butterflies all along the sides of them because the first day I can remember, a monarch landed on the tip of her shoe. We've loved them ever since, so whenever one of us wants to get something sentimental it usually involves the butterfly. It's a bit quirky, but it's our thing.

I go stand next to her in the mirror, to admire the outfit she picked out for me. It's a pair of my favourite ripped jeans that are covered with a lot of flowers and butterflies that I've drawn and a super cute, cropped band tee that I thrifted myself. This is one of the reasons why I love Sadie so much; she will never hold back when telling you your style sucks, but she always knows exactly what you like to wear.

We have this little tradition that every first day of school we take a Polaroid to stick to my wall of pictures, so I grab the camera that's sitting by my bedside table and capture the last first day of school.

She looks over at me and asks if I'm ready. I nod my head yes, but I can't bear the feeling that this year is not going to end the way we want it to. As Sadie grabs her bag and heads downstairs, I tape the picture to my wall. I stand in front of the wall admiring it for a few seconds until I hear my mom's voice calling out for me,

"Sweetie, come down for breakfast. There won't be anything left if you take too long,"

"Coming Mom," I call back.

I back away from my wall and grab my book bag. As I make my way downstairs, I can't help but smell the delicious breakfast my mom has created. I smell the sweetness of the pancakes and the salty aroma of freshly cooked…

"BACON!" We rarely get bacon in this house, so when we have it, it's usually a treat. Or something horrible happened and my parents are trying to ease the mood. The second I sat down at the table; I could tell this wasn't a 'just because we love you' situation. This is an 'I know you don't need a soulmate, but we strongly believe that you should make an effort to find one' type of conversation.

"I don't know how many times I have to tell you guys this, but I don't want to find my soulmate."

"We know sweetie, but your mom and I think you should at least try to make a connection with someone this year."

"Kayleigh, we only want what's best for you, and being sent to the Bunker is not that."

"Can I remind you guys that nobody knows what happens in the Bunker? Maybe it is the best thing that could happen."

"You realize, no one has ever come out of the Bunker, right?"

"Yeah so? Maybe it's so good that no one wants to come back out."

I can tell by the look on their faces, that they do not find this amusing. They all seem very freaked out by the whole idea of being taken away and never being heard from again.

"Sadie? Help me out here a little."

"Sorry Kayls, but I agree with your parents. I don't want to lose my best friend."

"Well, you're still gonna have Alec, so you'll be just fine," it comes off snarkier than I had hoped.

"You know that's different. Alec's my soulmate, I'm kinda stuck with him now."

"Yeah, the soulmate that you met when you were like 5 five years old."

It was like love at first sight for them. Sadie was playing on the swings while Alec was playing in the sand. They made eye contact and have been inseparable ever since. It turned out they really were soulmates so, no Bunker for them.

Essentially how the whole system works is if you think you've met your soulmate before the deadline you can do this test that tells you if they are your soulmate or not. If you pass, then you get to keep living your life with your soulmate, if not...

There are essentially three ways for you to be sent to the bunker:
1. ***Fail your test on the day of the deadline.***
2. ***Fail your test on an earlier day (for a maximum of two tries)***
3. ***Or declare that you have not found your soulmate.***

I plan to go with the third option.

Most people take the test before the final day, giving them ample time to find someone else in case the first one doesn't work out. It's honestly the safest bet, but you only have two tries before you get sent to the Bunker. That's what my parents did and that's what Sadie and Alec did a couple of summers ago.

The rest of breakfast kinda goes by rather quickly. I try to tune everyone out when they start talking about all the soulmate stuff because I hate thinking about it. At around 8 o'clock, Sadie and I get into her vintage blue Bronco, we take down the roof and start blasting the music, as we pull out of the driveway.

Chapter 2

Kayleigh

The drive over to Alec and Kate's house flies by in an instant. We've been picking him and his twin sister up for school almost every day since Sadie finally got access to her car. Don't get me wrong, she is a very safe driver, now. She failed her first time taking the practical, but she still claims that it was not her fault. She saw a sale in some department store and kind of swerved into a tree. It was not her finest move, but she managed to pass the second time behind the wheel.

As we start pulling into their driveway, I see the two of them walking toward the car. Alec is towering over his sister by at least a foot. If you didn't already know they were siblings, you would not be able to tell. Alec has this olive-like skin tone, with sage green eyes, and dark black hair. He is wearing an outfit that Sadie probably picked out for him the night before because he genuinely looks presentable today. Usually, he is wearing grey athletic pants with a black dry-fit t-shirt. Alec is on the high school's baseball team, so he is in pretty good shape. I would never admit that to him, but he is. He's tall, and lean, with the perfect amount of definition in his muscles.

Sadie has been trying to convince me to go watch a few games with her, but it is not my type of crowd. I do end up going in the end, but I try not to pay too much attention. I do remember her saying he was the catcher for the team though. She says he is the best one on the team, but that's just the girlfriend in her talking. From what I hear around school the title for all-star of the team goes to Spencer Brown. King of the jocks, and winner of the "I'm the biggest ass" award. He is dating, none other than Josie Carson. She and I used to be best friends, but one day she just woke up and decided to hate me forever. So, she made it her life goal to ruin my mine, lucky me.

Kate eventually reaches the car window and gives it a subtle knock. I jump out of the car and let them take their seats in the back and we start heading to school, and I look up into the rearview mirror.

"I still don't understand how you guys are even related."

"Well," Alec starts to say, "when a man and a woman fall in love, they get together and make this thing called a baby. After a while, this baby leaves the mother's stomach and grows into a rather attractive young man. But in our case, this little shit next to me, followed me out."

I turn around to slap Alec, but Kate has already beat me to it. "Thank you so much for the quick lesson on how babies are made, I never would've known without you telling me," I add.

Alec rubs his arm and winks at me, "Anytime little Kay."

"Bro, I swear, you better stop with that nickname. I'm not even that small."

"Whatever you say little Kay," he says behind a snicker.

He's been calling me little Kay for as long as I could remember. It doesn't even make sense, I'm not the smallest one in the friend group. But it pisses me off just enough that he keeps doing it. I seriously should not give him the satisfaction, but it just boils my blood.

Kate quickly chimes in before this argument lasts all day,

"Honestly Kay, I think that to myself all the time. How could someone as smart as me, be related to someone as stupid as Alec," she says as a grin appears on her face.

We all burst into laughter after hearing what Kate said. But in all seriousness, they look nothing alike. Kate has shoulder-length blonde hair, with bright blue eyes. She stands at a whopping 5 foot 4 and has the biggest dimples you could imagine. Her face is covered with freckles, while Alec's face is always clear, even when he spends all summer out in the sun. They barely look like siblings let alone twins.

Without the usual bickering between Alec and whoever else is in the car, the silence in the car starts to bother me a little, so I crank up the music that's been quietly playing in the background. Alec tries recommending some new rap song he heard over the summer, but no one ever messes with my morning music. We spend the rest of the car ride singing our lungs out to one of Avicii's many songs. It's perfect timing because just as the song is finishing up, we pull into Sadie's parking spot, which just so happens to be next to Reed River's spot. He is just leaning up against his ride by the time Sadie turns the ignition off.

Reed is Kate's soulmate. He is also on the high-school baseball team but plays center field. He usually wears a baseball cap to school, but today he has his brown fluffy hair soaking up all the sun. He has more colour on him than normal, which doesn't come as too much of a surprise, since he did spend all summer with Alec. He is just as tall as Alec, maybe even a couple of inches taller. Reed is built a bit smaller than Alec, but his muscles are just as defined. Both guys look like they are straight out of a movie. But again, I can't let them know that, or they would never shut up about it. I used to have this big crush on Reed when we were little kids, but I quickly got over it when he and Kate found out they were each other's soulmates. Alec and Reed are best friends, so when Alec found out about Kate and Reed seeing each other, he was a little annoyed. Ended with a couple of black eyes, but they made up rather quickly.

So, for as long as I could remember it's been me fifth wheeling with everyone else. They never make me feel uncomfortable though, we've all just been friends for so long I'm practically their sister.

We all start heading into school when the most obnoxious car comes rolling into the parking lot. It's the new four-seater white convertible Audi and it belongs to Josie, and her little boy toy Spencer just tags along. They pull into the first parking spot almost knocking over an unsuspecting freshman.

In less than two fucking seconds, there's a swarm of high school kids surrounding the car. Spencer climbs out of the car to greet his fellow jock bros, while Josie touches up her caked-on clown makeup in the rearview mirror.

When she finally finishes with her makeup, Josie makes her way out and around her car where she spots me and my friends. She stops right in front of Spencer and lays one hell of a kiss on him, that he wasn't even expecting it.

"Well, I guess this is my time to go jump off a building," I say with my most sarcastic voice.

Sadie nudges me slightly and giggles. "Oh, come on, they're kinda cute together."

"If by 'kinda cute' you mean, the most nauseating thing to look at, then yes Sadie, you are correct. They are just adorable."

Sadie rolls her eyes, and we lock arms. The school bell rings, and my friends and I make our way into the building for our final first day of high school.

Chapter 3
SPENCER

I can feel everybody's eyes piercing through my skin. Most of the time, I think Josie just does shit like this for attention, but with the way she's kissing me right now, there is no doubt in my mind that this girl is in love with me. Her hands begin to curl around the soft spot on my neck and I'm not one to shy away from PDA, I don't really care what people think of me. Being the captain of the baseball team comes with a lot of attention whether I like it or not. Plus, I'm a fantastic kisser, so why deprive the world of seeing me in action?

The second Josie pulls away from the kiss, my boys are quick with their whistles.

"All right show is over," she says while grabbing her Marc Jacobs tote bag from the backseat of her car.

She holds her bag out waiting for me to take it.

"Will you hold it for me babe? You know how tired I get when I must hold such heavy things."

With the adorable puppy dog eyes that she has perfected over the years, and the smoking hot kiss she just laid on me, how can I say no?

"Anything for you baby." Maybe that shouldn't have been my immediate response because the guys standing around us give me a subtle look of disappointment. They all seem to think that Josie has me wrapped around her finger.

They might be right, but this girl works extremely hard for it if you know what I mean. Before Josie and I even got together, I was the king of the school. I'm captain of the varsity baseball team, I essentially have a 4.0 GPA and anyone who is anyone just gravitates towards me. The girls and gays love me, the jocks want to be me, I'm nice to the losers so they do what I want, and don't get me started on the freshman. It's like I have these little minions at my beck and call, they do whatever I want whenever I want. It's the perk of being 'the man' on campus.

I wouldn't consider any of them my best friend. Don't get me wrong I got a lot of friends but none I would trust with deep shit.

But seriously who cares, I'm Spencer Brown for fuck's sake. Who at this school would hate me?

As I turn to walk into the school, I feel this sudden jolt in my back. Some chick just walked straight into me and dropped her entire book bag. I go to help her pick it up but Josie steps in.

"Watch where you're going, freak," barks my girlfriend.

"Wow Josie, so very original of you, did you come up with it all by yourself," says the girl.

"Whatever loser, no one likes you anyways."

"Oh no, my whole day is ruined," the girl says sarcastically, "whatever will I do if everyone hates me?"

I can't hold back my laughter, which immediately results in daggers coming from Josie's eyes.

This girl has hit a nerve in Josie because she looks even more upset than she did when I dropped my drink on one of her designer sweaters. Let me tell you, that was not a fun day.

Josie hurries me towards the opening of the school, while the girl that ran into me kept picking up her things.

"What was that about?" I ask hesitantly.

"What do you mean babe?"

"With that girl back there? She didn't do anything wrong."

"Trust me, sweetie, that girl is bad news."

I look back in her direction, and I see her talking with a few of my baseball teammates. I swear I've never seen her before, but I feel like I've known her my whole life.

"She doesn't look like bad news."

"Spencer! Just listen to me, Kayleigh Harris, is the biggest bitch on the planet."

"Kayleigh Harris?" That name sounds way too familiar, but I can't seem to put my finger on it.

"Yes, Kayleigh Harris, my former best friend from when we were kids." Josie can tell I'm still not understanding who she is. "The girl who ruined my life. She's been going to school with us for years. Come on Spence, I've talked about her so many times."

"Oh, Kayleigh Harris, of course, I remember." I still have no idea what she's talking about but sometimes it's better to just agree. But even though I can't remember who she is, I seriously feel like I've known this girl forever.

Weird.

"Good," says Josie, "now let's get to class before some wannabe takes my seat."

I grab my girlfriend by her waist, and we head through the doors, for our final first day of school.

Chapter 4

SPENCER

We walk into our first-period class, it just so happens to be my favourite course of the semester, AP Biology with Mrs. Walters. She is by far my favourite teacher, and she's the only person who truly knows how smart I am. She's been helping me figure out what I am going to do once I get out of high school.

Not many people know this, but I desperately want to be a veterinarian, I've only ever told my parents, Mrs. Walters, and Josie, but she never seems to care, so I've stopped talking about it with her. I've dreamt of helping animals ever since I was a little kid. I usually don't bring it up in conversation because the kids I hang with, don't vibe very well with the "smart kids". They're all just assholes who think they will go pro one day, so I just let them live in their fantasy world.

This AP class has loads of labs for us to do, so on the first day of class we usually find out who are lab partner will be, and we stay with them all semester. I find my name on the list and notice that I'm sitting right in the front. I don't mind this at all, because now I'll be able to listen to what the teacher is saying, but Josie seems to be a little agitated.

She looks for her name and notices that she is all the way in the back. It makes sense though; Mrs. Walters strongly dislikes Josie. If I'm being honest, she isn't the smartest person I've met but I don't fault her for it. Everyone has the things they're good at. Hers, however, are limited to popularity, cheerleading, and shopping.

Class is starting, and my partner is still not here. I hadn't even thought to check the rest of the list to see if anyone is even next to me. Maybe Mrs. W thinks I could do the labs on my own. Fuck yeah. Mrs. W thinking I'm good enough to do the labs on my own is the biggest compliment someone can ask for. She rarely lets students be by themselves unless they are at the top of the class.

Does she really have that much faith in me?

Just as the door is about to close, the girl that ran into me outside strolls in. My hopes of Mrs. Walters thinking I'm the strongest student fades as I look around the class and see that the only available seat left … is right next to me.

Oh shit. This could not be worse.

"Great, nice of you to join us, Kayleigh," says Mrs. Walters. The girl slightly smiles. "Right in the front next to Spencer."

I can see the eye roll forming in slow motion, the second she notices that it's me sitting next to her. I try not to feel offended, but I can't help but feel my ego break a little.

"Hi, I'm Spencer, but everyone just calls me Spence." She looks at me as if I'm the devil reincarnate.

"I know who you are, thanks," she says with the out most disgust.

"Ouch, ok" I reply. "Something tells me you aren't my biggest fan?"

"How long did that take you to figure out?" she says in a sarcastic tone.

"Only a few seconds really," I say with my most uplifting voice.

She rolls her eyes for the second time. I take that as my cue to stop talking. Thank God, Mrs. Walters is just about ready to start class because, with the amount of tension between me and this girl, I would be surprised if we both make it out of this class alive.

Kayleigh

I cannot believe, I got paired up with this jackass, for my favourite class. I literally would've rather been partnered up with Lord Voldemort, than deal with the ego that is Spencer Brown.

He even had the nerve to introduce himself, as if we haven't been in the same fucking school since we were 3 years old.

Doesn't surprise me though, usually the assholes of the grade stick together and don't veer far from the popular crowd.

I try not to let Spencer ruin my favourite class, so I try and listen to Mrs. Walters's introduction before I look over the schedule that has already been passed out.

I grab the piece of paper that is laying on the desk, and I start to read it over, when all of a sudden, I could feel the ice-cold breath of my lab partner breathing down my neck. I turn to him with the most gracious smile.

"Can I help you?"

"No, you're good, just trying to look at the schedule."

"Well, do you mind leaning the other way, because I can smell the coffee you had for breakfast?"

"Actually, smartass, it was an iced chai latte if you had to know. And it was delicious."

"Oh my god, an iced chai latte? Did they write your name on the cup with a whole bunch of hearts also?"

I'm now looking at him with puppy dog eyes, just so he can tell I don't expect a response from him.

"Damn, you really are gonna be a tough lab partner."

"Oh, I'm sorry, I really didn't want to make this year hard for you," I say with a pout.

Mrs. Walters clears her throat in our direction.

"Spencer and Kayleigh, if you two are done sharing your coffee orders, can I please get back to my course description?"

We both nod our heads and face forward.

Spencer leans towards me and says, "Kayleigh? I expected your name to be something a little more demonic, like Satan, or Bellatrix."

"How funny because I would rather be partnered with Voldemort than have to deal with you all semester," I say with an even bigger smile.

"He who shall not be named, is better than me?" asked Spencer.

I give him a quick nod before the bell rings to announce the end of the class. I've packed my things rather quickly but I'm still not fast enough to get out of here before I face the wrath of Spencer's girlfriend. The screech of her voice reaches us before I even get out of my seat.

"Babe! Hurry up, my books aren't gonna carry themselves."

"Wow, your girlfriend is beckoning. Best not be late."

"Thanks, Satan, what will I ever do without you?"

"Not sure, but hopefully we find out soon."

Before Josie can attack me from behind, I call out to Mrs. Walters, to discuss seating arrangement quickly.

"Hi Kayleigh, what can I do for you?"

"Hi Mrs. Walter, I was wondering if there was any way to change lab partners for the year. I don't see how I can work with Spencer for the entire semester."

"Normally I would switch people if there were serious concerns Kayleigh, but there aren't any other spaces for you to move to."

"What if you switch me with the royal bitch?"

"As much as we both dislike Josie, you know you can't refer to other students like that. Both you and Spencer have the highest grades from any class I have ever thought, I have a feeling you two will do very well together this semester."

"Spencer? Spencer Brown? The kid who is sitting next to me has good grades in Biology? You cannot be serious, right?"

"People can surprise you, Kayleigh, just give him a chance. Now I really must leave, there is a faculty meeting in the board room. See you next class."

"Thank you, Mrs. Walters."

I look over to Josie, Spencer and the rest of their posse giggling over something someone said. I try my hardest not to vomit on the spot and make my way out the door as quickly as possible. Thank God Sadie and Reed are waiting for me when I'm finished with class.

Before I even get there, I can see their smiles. "Don't even think about it," I say without even stopping.

The two of them break out into laughter, "This could not be more perfect, you and Spencer Brown having to spend all year together." He eventually gets the sentence out in between his laughter. I'm too livid to come up with a sarcastic remark. *This rarely happens.*

I intertwine my arms in theirs and we make our way to the next class. I try giving them my signature "don't start with me" look but they are too far gone to even realize.

Chapter 5

Kayleigh

The sound of the PA system turns on

"Welcome back students of Midrock Falls High. We hope you all spent your summer wisely, and hope you are ready for another amazing year. Two quick PSAs, join a club day will begin after the final bell this afternoon, please make sure to sign up for your clubs. And secondly, we want to wish all seniors luck in finding their soulmates. This a reminder that May 4th is the final day to declare soulmates, and all those who do not will be sent to the Bunker. Once again, we wish you all the best of luck and hope you have an amazing school year."

"And time. It took a total of 3 hours and 17 minutes before we were reminded that everyone is required to fit into the societal norm of finding a soulmate. It is ridiculous that as a society we have deemed it necessary to find someone who will constantly be by your side."

"Thank you so much Kayls, for once again reminding us that you don't have a soulmate."

"Seriously little Kay, some people don't mind the soulmate thing."

"Coming from two people who have had their soulmate since they can practically walk, yeah I wonder why you don't care all that much."

Don't get me wrong, I will always be pro don't need a soulmate but being in a group of friends who have no reason to ever worry about the Bunker really strikes a nerve. I have never been afraid of the Bunker, I've made peace with the fact that I'm not looking for the soulmate, but there's still the little voice in my head wondering what happens behind the closed doors.

No one has ever come out of the Bunker, which is kind of strange considering everyone who does not find their soulmate ends up there. So, in theory, you should find your soulmate but the whole government thing is stupid and makes no sense regardless. My family has only ever had one person go there. My aunt Victoria. She was my age when she went.

My mom talked a lot about her when I was little, but as I grew up, I reminded her a lot of her sister, so she stopped telling me stories. Maybe when I go there, I'll see her.

I see Kate's hand waving in front of my face.

"Earth to Kayleigh, you there?"

I snap back to reality. "Sorry, I was thinking about something."

"You do that so often, that you'd think I'd be used to it by now."

"Anyways," Sadie says "have we decided which club we were gonna join this year? I was thinking we could all be cheerleaders."

"For sure Sades, that's the one thing I want to do, go out and cheer for the jocks of the school."

"Excuse you Kayls, Reed and I are those jocks."

"I stand corrected, we would be cheering for the jocks and the bench warmers," I break out laughing.

That struck a nerve with them both.

"On a serious note, I think I'm going to either join the art club or the after-school vet program. I hear it's new and think it could be fun."

"That's such a good idea! You'll be great at it."

"Thank you!"

SPENCER

"… Once again we wish you all the best of luck and hope you have an amazing school year."

"Hi, my handsome boyfriend," says Josie as she sits on my lap. I wrap my arms around her waist and look her in the eyes.

"Tell me again why we have to wait until May 4th to do the soulmate test?"

"Because silly, that's what we decided on, remember."

"I remember you telling me that you wanted to wait until the last possible day, but never told me why."

"Don't worry about it, everything will work out in the end, I promise," she says this with a slight smirk, but before I can respond, she's already pressing her lips onto mine like no one is watching. By the time she pulls away, I forget what we were talking about moments prior. I am absolutely in love with this girl, and she knows it.

"So," I say looking at her, "what club are you going to join, I was thinking of doing the new after-school vet program."

With no hesitation, she breaks out laughing. "You can't be serious, my boyfriend the captain of the baseball team is going to join the vet program? Yeah right."

"Babe, I'm serious. I really think it could be fun."

"Don't come running to me when it's too much for you. I'll be on the cheer squad for the fifth year in a row."

She is very dismissive when it comes to the things I enjoy doing. To her everything is superficial, if it doesn't boost your popularity in any way, it does not matter. I guess that comes with the idea that the mayor of Midrock Falls is her father. He is the king of winning popularity contests.

For as long as I could remember her family has always been in the position of power. Whether it was her dad, or her grandfather, the mayor has always been a Carson. There is no longer a point in voting for a mayor, no one ever runs against the Carson family, so they always win on a technicality.

Josie does make a good point though, with all the AP classes I'm taking, the baseball team, and now the vet program, it may be a lot more time than I anticipated, but I'm willing to put the work in. I also try to never tell her that I agree with her on something, because I will never hear the end of it. She tends to hold on to things, and me telling her she is right is one of those things you try and avoid.

Chapter 6

SPENCER

I never could have imagined my last season playing on the Knights. This will be my fourth year starting, my third year as captain, and hopefully my fourth championship but let's not get too carried away, we still have the whole season to go.

My pre-practice routine is pretty much set in stone, I walk onto the field the exact same way I have for the last three years, headphones on full-blast, blue Gatorade in my right hand and eye black already dripping down my face from the heat. I stop just before the entrance to the field, to take it all in, one more time. The smell of freshly cut grass, the feeling of the sun beaming down on my face, and the dust cloud forming by my feet, has never felt more perfect.

I'm always the first one on the field before every practice, and every game, it's some stupid superstition I've developed over the years. At first, I just showed up super early to make sure I got onto the field first, but now the team just hangs back till I get out there, that's just another perk of being captain, I guess.

My foot hovers over the field, and as I am about to take my first step onto the sand, I freeze. This tall lanky dude is running laps around the field half-hour before practice is called for. *Half hour before the practice is called for! What dumbass shows up this early?* I immediately begin to panic, my final season is going to be a disaster, I haven't even touched the field yet and it's ruined. Every worst-case scenario is playing in my head one after another. *How do I let this asshole beat me to the field?* I stand still for what felt like forever. *It was only five seconds.* My pump music slowly fades away, and I hear two teammates laughing behind me. At first, I thought they were just laughing at each other, but I realized they were laughing at me.

How sweet, my teammates find joy in my misery.

I only turn around when I feel a hand pressed onto my shoulder, I see Alec Rose, the green-eyed god, and Reed Rivers the second-most athletic kid in school. We have been playing ball together from the very beginning. The three of us were the only freshmen to make the team when we started. Both guys are super well-liked, but they usually just chill with their small group of friends. If it weren't for the whole soulmate thing, these two guys would be my biggest competition in the girl's department. *Now that's hard to admit.* All anyone can ever talk about is how Reed Rivers has the most perfectly toned body, with his brown fluffy hair that always seems to be styled just right, and how Alec looks like a demigod who has the personality of a golden retriever puppy.

I'm perfectly content with my masculinity so I'm just gonna say it. If I were a girl, I would also be all over them.

The two of them have been inseparable since they were born. Their mothers were best friends and had them only a few days apart, and ever since then they've been best friends. They are basically brothers and will do almost anything for each other. One practice during our freshman year, the boys were hazing Reed for something stupid he had done. The poor kid was so embarrassed, he ran off the field. Alec didn't even hesitate. He threw jabs at the seniors about everything: their game, their girls, and their moms. I was in absolute shock by the time he finished roasting them. A few minutes later, Reed came back out and everything was forgotten. I never had a friend like that. *I always wanted a friend like that, but never really found one.* I like to think I'm friends with everyone at the school, but I do wish I had a connection with someone like them. For anyone thinking Josie is my person…as much as I love her, and don't get me wrong I do, but she is not one to give good advice. Unless that advice involves styling a vintage purse, you are shit out of luck.

"What's up Spence? You look a little lost." Alec chirps behind a grin.

"Who the fuck is taking the field this early?" I say as I'm pointing towards the moving figure. "And don't you even dare say, me." I quickly add.

He throws his hands up in protest. He points out to the moving figure, "That's Colin, coach said he was a transfer this year and apparently he's a solid player."

"Is he a senior?"

"Yes, he is."

I can feel the colour fading from my face. This Colin kid is giving me a bad feeling, and clearly it shows cause the guys are quick to respond.

"It's just some stupid superstition cap, don't let that get to you," Reed adds as he nudges me towards the opened gate.

"Yeah, guess y'all are right. I've been at this long enough; I can kick his ass in my sleep."

"Now we're talking. You want to go toss a few with me and Alec before the rest of the team shows?"

"Oh, for sure, you guys can help me figure out some form of punishment for the new guy," I say somewhat jokingly walking onto the field.

...

Practice went by quickly, and I'm not gonna lie, it wasn't my best. I missed a few routine flies, and the batting just wasn't spectacular, plus I got knocked in the head by a throw from the new guy. I swear to God he did it on purpose. No one who plays ball at this level, misthrows by that much. This just means that his punishment will be a lot worse than what I had originally planned. Me, Alec, and Reed decided that he will be walking up to the plate with the Barbie theme song playing in the background, and just to spice things up even more, after the game he needs to perform for the team in the locker room. I can't wait to see him bring out his inner Barbie girl.

Baseball and cheer practice always end around the same time, so when I finish up on the field, I make my way to the gym to get Josie. She's already waiting for me in the bleachers, with her three duffels that have her initials embroidered on the side of it. She seems very in tune with something on her phone, I even see her giggle a few times. The moment she looks up and notices me walking towards her, the good humor fades. I try letting it go, but I can't help my curiosity.   As I go to reach for her bags, I ask her what was so funny.

"Oh nothing, just a video Sabrina sent me."

One thing I have learnt since I've been with Josie is that she has certain tells. You know how some people avoid eye contact or smile when they lie? Well, Josie refuses to look at me, and proceeds to play with a piece of her hair. I know this girl is lying, so I press as much as I can as we make our way to the car.

"What type of video was it?"

"Just some cheer fails from a group we used to compete against. Why are you so interested babe?"

"No reason, you just looked cute giggling when I walked towards you."

"Cute?" She stops in her tracks, "I think you've misspoken; I assure you I looked hot," she says as she flips her hair to the back of her head. I let out a quick puff of air and chuckle,

"My bad, you looked extra hot."

We eventually reach Josie's car, and at the end of the day, she usually gets too tired to drive home, so I get behind the wheel. I go to put her bags in the backseat but remember that my girl is a princess, so I run around to the passenger door to open it. Only then, do I make my way around to the driver's side and get settled.

I put the car in drive and head towards the parking lot exit. The drive home is normally fifteen minutes, so it gives us plenty of time to catch up.

"So, how was practice?"

"It was horrible! The new girls trying out were horrendous. They can barely do the tumbling required and have little to no voice for the cheers. There was one decent girl and coach loved her, so did the other girls, but something was off about her. She was able to do everything I could, and coach even joked about her taking my spot. As if she could ever do that."

"I'm sure your coach was just trying to light a fire under your ass. Get you guys more competitive?"

"Well, if she thinks I'm worried that some freshman is gonna come and take my spot my last year as cheer captain, she has another thing coming."

"You know you turn me on when you get like this."

She turns to me and smiles, but that quickly fades. She then brings decides to bring up the seating arrangements from this morning's biology class.

"I cannot believe Mrs. Walters sat that bitch next to you in AP bio," she groans, "I specifically asked my daddy to get us in the same class so I can spend more time with you. I don't even like biology."

"It's not that big of a deal, it's only for a few hours when we have labs."

"So what? Do you like sitting next to her? Have you not heard me at all? I fucking hate that girl, she is the absolute worst thing to ever walk the planet. I vowed that I would make the rest of her short life a living hell. The Bunker already has a spot waiting for her."

"I mean, I know you don't like her, but you never told me why." I let that linger before adding, "She must've done something horrible, but there's no reason to be jealous or hope that she doesn't find her soulmate." Maybe I shouldn't have added the jealousy part because the glare that I'm currently receiving can send anybody to an early grave.

"Are you fucking kidding me, Spencer. Do you honestly believe that I'm jealous of that two-timing bitch? The whole soulmate thing is just the icing on the cake cause if she doesn't find hers then I never have to see her again."

"You seem a little jealous," I say shyly, "How are you going to mess with her soulmate?"

"Well, you're wrong, I am not jealous, I just hate her. And if my boyfriend truly loved me, he would hate her also, and at least try to get his fucking seat changed," she growls, "Did you forget that my father is the mayor of this town, he has access to all the soulmate pairings, and I'm his little princess, so I've seen her file at least once."

"Babe come on; you are being a little over dramatic. I already overheard Kayleigh try and get the seats changed but Mrs. W shut that down." I reach over to grab Josie's thigh. "I promise you; I will not be friends with this girl. I only ever see her during bio and if it really means that much to you, I'll only talk to her if I'm on fire."

Before she says another word I quickly add, "But don't you think messing with her soulmate is a little much though? Won't her soulmate also be sent down to the Bunker if he doesn't find her?"

"It's collateral damage, anyway, whoever is destined to be with that bitch deserves the same punishment."

"Damn, I never realized how much you've thought about this."

"Whatever."

We finally pull into her long roundabout driveway that leads to the biggest house in town, 223 Brook Valley. Considering they are only four people living in the house, I don't understand why they need so much space, but I guess being the mayor comes with a lot of perks. Before we get out of the car, I tell Josie that our usual Thursday night dates will have to be moved to Saturday, because I signed up to be a volunteer at the vet clinic. She was pissed off at first but then got a text from someone and she was fine. I tried asking her who it was from, but she quickly diverted the question with a kiss.

I'm a sucker for that. Anytime she presses those lips to mine I lose all train of thought. It's like a cheat code she's figured out, I'm not complaining, but I should really get better at it. Can't have her thinking that she has all the power in the relationship.

Chapter 7
Kayleigh

Me: I'm here.

Me: Waiting in the car.

Me: Hello!!??

Me: SADIE ALEXIS SILVERSTEIN THIS IS NOT FUNNY

IF U DON'T HURRY UP!!!!

Sades: geez sorry babes.

Sades: I'm coming now.

Me: good!

Me: Bring me something to eat as punishment lol.

Sades: kk I'll go grab the fruit snacks.

Me: thx :)

Usually, Sadie is much quicker in the morning, so having to wait ten minutes is asking for a lot. It doesn't help that we still need to go pick up Kate and Alec. My biggest pet peeve is being late, but now that we are seniors it doesn't matter as much, I still hate it though.

Sadie finally strolls into the front seat of my car carrying a handful of my favourite fruit snacks.

"Holy shit Sadie, you took forever!"

"Ugh, don't remind me I slept through my first alarm, so I rushed to get ready. Please tell me you didn't take out my emergency get-ready kit."

Before Sadie even got her license, I was the designated driver for the group, so over time she started leaving her crap all over my car. One day I just went out to buy her a small tote bag, just so she can leave it in my car. It has come in handy several times, so I never took it out. I start to pull out of the driveway, as I point to the glove compartment just by her feet.

"Thank god!"

Sadie starts rummaging through the compartment until she pulls out the small bag. I designed the front of it when I was in my band tee graphic phase, so the tote is covered with lyrics from all my favourite old-time bands. She looks through the bag and quickly finds what she is desperately looking for just as I pull into Alec and Kate's driveway.

I get only one honk off by the time the two of them come stumbling out of the house. You can easily tell that Alec is not a morning person. His hair covers half of his face, his eyes are extremely puffy, and he is carrying an overly large bottle, that's filled to the rim with iced coffee. Kate, on the other hand, loves morning. She walks to the car with so much energy that just makes her glow. You'd think she was awake for hours. Her outfit is perfectly put together, a white floral skirt that lays just above her knee, with her signature pink halter top that Reed got her for their two-year anniversary. She is wearing the cutest pair of black covers, to match the black satin bow holding her hair back, and to top it all off, she is carrying an adorable shoulder bag.

I absolutely love Kate's style, it's very similar to Sadie's but also quite different, they both got this chic girly look. It's a good mix of summer girl and dainty. My style is the complete opposite. I tend to go with the whole band tee shirts, jeans, and the occasional skirt. I sometimes, *very rarely*, let them dress me up, so on the rare occasion I will throw on a mini red summer dress. Surprisingly, red looks amazing on me. Whenever I look to add colour to my outfit, it's either red or blue. They bring out all my good features.

When Alec opens the car you can immediately see him wake up.

"Holy shit Sadie, how much perfume did you spray in here?"

I hadn't even noticed the smell until Alec brought it up.

"Come on, you're overreacting. It's not that bad."

"No Sades, I'm gonna have to agree with Alec on this one," I try reaching for the window.

"Seriously Sadie, it smells like you dumped the whole bottle out in the car," adds Kate.

That must have been what she was looking for.

Alec is quick to say, "Little Kay, can you open the windows any slower, I think I'm going to suffocate back here, if I have to smell my girlfriend any longer."

He makes these gagging sounds that cause me and Kate to burst out laughing.

In her most sarcastic tone, Sadie laughs. "You are so lucky that we are late for school and that I love you because otherwise, you would be walking."

"That's a great idea babe, maybe then I could breathe again," he says with a smile.

As I put the car into drive, I lean to turn the volume up so I can drown out this back-and-forth convo the love birds have going on. Knowing them they could do this all-fucking day, so I play my usual morning playlist and try to ignore them.

By the time I turn into the school parking lot, we've all have been singing along to whatever song is next in the queue. The songs that come on range in genre, which makes it the best playlist, if I do say so myself. We went from Before He Cheats by the great Carrie Underwood, to Happily by the band that's been on hiatus for far too long, One Direction. I know these songs seem to be basic, but this mix I put on, is the one for when I'm with other people. It has a bit of what everyone likes.

I pull into our shared parking spot, right next to wear Reed is patiently waiting. He usually gets here around the time we do but because of how long Sadie took this morning, he's been standing there for a few minutes. The bell still hasn't rung so we aren't as late as we thought we were.

He makes his way around the car to Kate's side to open her door. I will say it over and over, Reed Rivers is the picture-perfect boyfriend. He's the type of guy you read about in books. He is tall, smart, athletic, funny, and just an all-around a nice person. He has this charm that makes people flustered, whenever they are near him. Guys like him just don't really exist anymore. Reed and Kate make a perfect couple. They are so different but so similar at the same time. They share a few interests in common, but they are so supportive of each other, that they would be willing to do anything for one another. It's very funny to me that Kate's soulmate happened to be her twin brother's best friend. If that isn't straight from a book with a brother's best friend trope, I don't know what is.

I see Alec walk around the car to meet Reed and he quickly whispers something into his year that makes him look up laughing.

"So, Sadie," Reed starts "how does it feel smelling like the nearest Bath and Body Works threw up on you?"

At this point, Alec is wheezing at his best friend's comment, as if he didn't just come up with that himself.

"You know what Rivers," Sadie is glaring at them now, "tell your buddy who is dying of laughter, that he can kiss my ass."

Now both Reed and Alec and laughing hysterically, so Sadie grabs my arm, and we walk towards the front doors. We leave the two boys and Kate near the car, where we can still faintly hear their voices. I try very hard to hide my smile, but Sadie catches on. She sees me from the corner of her eye and can't help but laugh as well. We both know the perfume was strong, but we couldn't let the boys have the satisfaction of thinking they were funny. We'd never hear the end of it.

The start of the day is relatively easy, I only have one three-hour block Thursday mornings before lunch, and usually the teacher lets us leave a few minutes before class lets out. I meet back up with the rest of my friends by the big willow tree that sits in the middle of the school court ward. It's one of our favorite places and since not many people sit around there, it is usually private. The four of them are all already sitting there by the time I get to them. They are mid-conversation on how the girlfriends of the baseball players should be forced to watch all the home games. Even though Kate and Sadie go to almost every home game, they still put up a decent fight. When they notice me walking over, they can't help but ask.

"Kayls, what do you think?"

"What do I think about what?"

"The whole, girlfriends of the players should go to every home game during the season."

Out of the corner of my eye, I see Alec and Reed trying to persuade me to side with them. They have their hands pressed together and are giving me the corniest puppy dog eyes.

"I think the girlfriends should do whatever they want."

Reed throws his hands in the air, "why'd we ask Kayleigh?"

"Because asshat, she is a very smart girl who always sides with her bestie." Sadie is gleaming.

"No, you just picked her because she doesn't believe that a girlfriend should come out and support their boyfriend."

"Excuse me," I say trying to sound the most offended, "I go with them to some of your stupid home games and I'm not even a girlfriend. Plus, I hate baseball, it makes little to no sense."

Alec proceeds to say, "And we appreciate it very much." He nudges Reed, who sarcastically adds, "We love having you watch the games."

I roll my eyes, "I just love coming to spend lunch with you guys. It always brings me so much joy."

"Awe, I love spending time with you too," says Sadie. The sarcasm flies right over her head. She's known me far too long that my sarcasm no longer works on that girl, which is a bit concerning considering I breath sarcasm.

"Anyways" I start to speak, "I'm gonna need y'all to go home with Reed today."

"What makes you think I want to chauffeur these losers around?"

"LOSERS!" says Kate, who quickly turns to face her boyfriend from her usual position of lying down between his legs.

"Di-did I say losers?" He starts to wipe drops of sweat from his forehead. "I meant losers and my beautiful, intelligent, one-of-a-kind girlfriend."

She kisses him on the cheek and lies back down.

"On another note, I got an email saying I was accepted for the clinic volunteering program, and it starts today after school, so I'll have to go straight there."

"OMG, you got the volunteering spot?"

"Yeah! I just found out this morning. There were only two spots, but I still don't know who else is doing it. I'll find out later today"

Sadie says, "Hopefully it's not that bitch Josie."

"In what world would Josie ever do anything for another living being," mumbles Kate.

"Fair point," agrees Sadie, "hopefully it's someone who has a personality."

Alec joins in, "Hopefully it's your soulmate."

"You sound just like my parents. Soulmate this, soulmate that, when are people going to understand that I don't give a flying fuck for that stuff."

"I'm just saying Kay, the deadline is not far away and none of us want to lose you to the fucking Bunker."

"I still have plenty of time left, but I've come to terms with not finding my soulmate."

"Don't you feel a little bad for the guy who will also be sent down because he didn't find you?"

"I never really thought about that. But I've made up my mind, I will not conform to society's way of relationships."

"All I'm saying little Kay is that you should at least give it a chance if you meet the right person."

"If I say yes to keeping an open mind, will you guys stop talking about it?"

A unanimous yes echoes under the tree.

"Fine, then I will keep an open mind."

They all look around at each other very pleased with themselves for getting me to agree to these circumstances. I'm letting you all know, that the chances of me finding someone is slim, but I'll do almost anything for my friends, so if "keeping an open mind" will make them happy, then that's what they'll think I'm doing.

Chapter 8
Kayleigh

Right when the final bell rings, I head straight to my car. I refuse to be late for my first shift at the clinic. It's maybe a fifteen-minute drive from school, so I get there with plenty of time to spare. The parking lot is basically deserted, so I assume the other student isn't here yet.

I decide to walk in a bit early, so I can introduce myself to the people who work there full-time. When I walk through the door I could hear bells jingle above my head, I look towards the front desk, and I see a woman maybe around 25 years old. She has jet black hair that is in a top knot bun. She has freckles all over her cheeks, a pair of glasses sitting on the top of her head, and a few pens hanging from her scrub top.

"Hi there, welcome to Dr. Patty's Paws, how can I help you?"

"Hi, my name is Kayleigh Harris. I'm one of the volunteers from Midrock Falls High."

"You're early! Dr. Patty's gonna love you. Let me go tell her you are here, and I'll bring you the scrubs you need wear."

"Thank you." She walks off towards the back.

A few minutes later, she walks back through the doors and hands me a set of purple scrubs.

"The bathrooms are just around the corner to your right."

I walk off in the direction of the bathrooms to change into my scrubs. They aren't the most flattering thing, but they'll have to do.

After I finally stop admiring myself in the mirror, I walk back out towards the front desk.

"I don't think I caught your name yet, Mrs.?"

"Please no need for formalities, I'm not even that much older than you. It's Lianne, pleasure to meet you."

"Nice to meet you too."

"If you want, you can take a seat just over there while you wait for Dr. Patty to be ready. She shouldn't be too long."

"Great, thanks."

It's a few minutes past the time I was intended to show up and still no sign of Dr. Patty or the kid from school. My impatience takes the best of me, and I decide to walk back up to Lianne to see if she needs help with anything.

"Is there anything I can help you with while I wait?"

"That's all right, it's been a pretty slow day."

"Okay, just let me know if you need anything." I did not feel like going back to sit in the waiting area so, I let a few seconds pass before asking her about the other volunteer.

"Let me check that for you." She flips through the papers on her desk until she pulls out a small yellow slip. "He put his initials instead of his name, he wrote S.B., and that he is a senior."

I try not to laugh but I can't help myself.

"S.B.? I don't think I know anyone with those initials."

I think through my class lists for few more seconds until I'm hit with the realization of who S.B. can be. I hope, I am wrong, but as soon as I hear the ring of the door opening, I can't bring myself to turn around. If I turn around, I'd have to come to terms with the fact that I will be spending every Thursday afternoon with…

"Hey, I'm one of the volunteers from Midrock Falls High. My name is Spencer Brown, but you can just call me Spence."

My heart sinks into my stomach.

"Hi Spence, I'm Lianne and this is…"

I turn around to face him. He flashes me this small when he realizes it's me.

"Satan? I can't believe you followed me here."

"I didn't follow you. If anything, you're the one who followed me."

"Whatever you say, sweetheart." He gives me a wink and runs his fingers through his hair.

I slightly shiver, "Don't ever do that again."

"Do what?"

"That whole winking thing."

"What winking thing."

"You are the most frustrating person I know."

He smiles and grabs the purple scrubs that Lianne placed on the counter. When he gets back from changing, Dr. Patty comes out to greet us both.

"You two must be my volunteers." She reaches her hand out towards the both of us.

"Yes, we are. This is Satan." He says that last part with a devilish grin and a little too much enthusiasm.

"Satan? I'm not sure I've heard that one before."

"He's joking," I quickly slap the side of his arm as hard as I can. "It's actually Kayleigh, sorry about him, he tends to mix up my name with his."

"I won't worry, I've known my nephew long enough, to realize when he is trying to crack some jokes."

I think my heart skips a beat.

"Your nephew?"

I turn my head towards Spencer, who's already gleaming. He is practically gloating at the fact that I just called him out in front of his aunt.

"My nephew," she replies. "Anyways let me bring you guys to the back where I will get you both started on something small."

Dr. Patty walks back through the doors she had first come out of. Before we follow, I turn to Spencer.

"You could've warned me that she was your aunt!" smoke is practically steaming from my ears, and my face has probably turned every shade of red possible. I am mortified.

"And miss this priceless reaction?" He takes out his phone and snaps a picture of my face. "I don't think I have ever seen anyone this red."

"You are such a jackass."

"Thank you," he takes a few steps towards me and whispers in my ear, "I try my best."

I roll my eyes and follow the path that Dr. Patty had taken. I quickly try to calm down before reaching her again, but it's quite hard knowing that Spencer is grinning from ear to ear right behind me.

After a quick tour of the clinic, all Dr. Patty has us do today is clean the back rooms. There are only three of them, so I decided that each of us will clean one by ourselves and do the last one together. I'm trying to keep our interactions to a minimum. There is no protest from Spencer, so I got right to it.

It took me around an hour to fully clean and restock the first room, and I thought I did a really good job on time, but when I walked into the third room, I saw Spencer sitting there reading a magazine.

He looks over towards me, "Holy shit Satan, what took you so long."

"What do you mean, I was done in an hour."

"An hour? To clean and restock a room?"

"Alright hot shot, how long did it take you?"

"About thirty minutes."

"Thirty minutes? Did you even clean it?"

"If you need some pointers feel free to ask."

"If you need some pointers feel free to ask," I say mockingly. "If you were done thirty minutes ago, why didn't you start this room?"

"You said we were going to do it together; I wasn't going to let you get away with not doing anything."

"Just shut up and help me finish this room."

Spencer gets off his chair and starts cleaning one side of the room while I restock the counters. Every now and then I "accidentally" push him, which really starts to tick him off. I do it a few more times for shits and giggles. Finding ways to piss him off is the only way I will ever survive spending this much time with him.

We finish everything in about twenty minutes, which is great because Dr. Patty said that when we were done, we could leave. It was a very short first day, but I'll take it.

We both walk back in the direction of Lianne's desk to get undressed and say goodbye. I make my way into the bathroom just as Patty comes out to the front to tell Spencer that she can give him a lift home if he wants to stay a few more hours till closing.

"Thanks for the offer, but I think I'm going to walk."

"Are you sure it's like an hour's walk, and it looks like it's going to rain."

"Don't worry about it, I'll turn it into a run so I can use it as a training day for baseball."

"Why don't you ask Kayleigh for a ride? She seems nice."

"No thank you, I rather walk in a tsunami. Plus, her nickname is Satan. Do you really want me getting in a car with here? I'll see you next week."

I walk out of the bathroom and see Dr. Patty waiting for me. I had overheard her conversation with Spencer and pray she doesn't bring it up.

"Thank you again, Dr Patty. If that's everything I guess, I'll see you next week."

"Actually, I have a favour to ask."

"Sure, what can I do?" *Fuck.*

"Do you happen to pass by Sycamore Lane on your way home?" *Should I lie?*

"Of course, it is actually right around the corner from me." *I should've lied.*

"That's great. Do you think you could give Spence a lift home, I was supposed to, but I have to stay a few more hours. He just walked out so he shouldn't have gotten too far."

How do you say, "No fucking way am I gonna take your nephew home?" without sounding rude. Here's how ... you don't.

"Sure, that shouldn't be a problem."

"Perfect. Thank you so much Kayleigh, see you next week!" She vanishes to the back room, and I think to myself how the hell did I get stuck taking home my least favourite person's boyfriend?

I get into my car and start driving down the street. Spencer must be a fast runner because he has gotten far by the time, I finally see him.

I roll down my window and scream towards him, "Your aunt asked me to take you home. Get in."

"Wow, Satan you really know how to make a guy feel so special."

"Don't be an ass. I'm the one in a car, and you're the one who is about to be drenched."

"I'm good. It's good exercise, and it's not even raining yet." Just as he says that the rain starts to fall, and a crash of thunder follows. Spencer practically lunges through the window.

I can't help but laugh. "Are you afraid of thunder?"

"No," he says, as he is shaking in the seat next to me.

"You totally are."

"No, I'm not, stop it. Can we just go?"

"Not until you admit it."

"Fine, fine you want to hear it." I nod my head. "I have a fear of thunder. There, you happy?"

"Very."

I start the car back up, and realize we have a twenty-minute drive ahead of us. There is no chance I will survive that long in complete silence, so I put on my queued playlist from this morning.

The first couple of songs play through, and then the unthinkable happens.

"I hate to break it to you Satan, but your music is trash." *He. Did. Not.*

It's a good thing we aren't on a busy road because I slam on the breaks jerking us both forwards.

"Get out of my car."

Spencer laughs.

"No need to get your panties in a bunch. Your music just isn't great."

"First of all, never talk about my panties again, and secondly who are you to judge my music taste."

"If I'm being honest with you, I thought you'd have more old-school stuff. Like Queen, The Rolling Stones, Led Zeppelin, shit I would've thought you'd at least have ABBA. Did you not wear a band tee to school the other day?"

"Not that I have to prove anything to you, those are reserved for my personal playlist." I play around with the radio till I see what I was looking for.

"So, why were we listening to overplayed, One Direction, and Taylor Swift?"

"First of all don't disrespect One Direction and Taylor like that. The playlist we were listening to is what I put on when I have other people in my car. My friends don't appreciate the music I prefer."

"Well, they have no taste."

For once I can agree with this twat.

"You're lucky you have good taste in music because if you criticized my music and had bad taste, you were walking the rest of the way… in the thunder." I slap the steering wheel as hard as I can, which causes a loud thumping sound. Spencer slightly jumps, which is the exact reaction I was looking for.

Spencer laughs a little to feel less embarrassed, not sure that worked well, but I just continue driving home. Unknowingly, we both start singing Gimme. Gimme. Gimme. by ABBA. It was quite enjoyable, but once the song came to an end we both realized what we were doing, and we agreed to not say anything about it. The rest of the ride home neither one of us spoke. If it weren't for the music we'd be sitting in complete silence.

Before I could even pull into his driveway, he gets a call. He reaches for the volume and shuts off my music. "What the fuck are you doing? Don't ever touch my music!" I almost scream at him. He then dares to shush me, in my own car.

"Hey babe, what's going on?" I can't hear the other end of the conversation, but I know he is talking to Josie.

"Yeah, it went well. Uh-huh... yeah... no she wasn't able to take me home... my aunt forced the other senior to take me home... no I don't think you know them..."

Clearly, he doesn't want to tell her I'm the other senior. I don't know if I should be offended or if he is doing it to save both of us from the headache.

"Ok... sure... I'll see you tomorrow... love you...bye."

"Seems to me like you're scared to tell your bitch that I'm the other senior."

"You don't need to call her a bitch, and plus, she fucking hates you. I'm saving the both of us from a headache by not telling her. You're welcome."

"Well, if she talks like a bitch and walks like a bitch, hate to break it to you but she's a bitch."

"You two really need to just kiss and make up."

"You would just love that won't you."

"Sure Satan, whatever you say."

That nickname is really starting to piss me off and I know he knows because every time he says it, he looks at my face for validation.

"Get out of my car jackass." *Jackass? Maybe that will stick.*

He opens the side door, hops out and closes the door again. Before walking away, he motions for me to roll the window down.

"Thanks for the ride."

"Yeah, whatever, I wasn't gonna say no to your aunt."

"I kinda figured you weren't simply doing it out of the goodness of your heart. Anyways thanks for the ride and I guess I'll see you in biology."

"Guess so."

I watch him go into his house, it's a habit I have, that I need to wait for the person to get inside safely, even if I very much dislike them. I couldn't just leave. When he gets in, I reverse out of the driveway and head home.

When I get into my house I tell my parents about my day, and quickly eat dinner, before I crash into bed. I don't even have the energy to call Sadie, to tell her about who my partner at the clinic is. She won't really care, so it can wait until tomorrow.

Chapter 9
SPENCER

Today is the season's home opener and the high school goes full out for the baseball team. It's a huge deal here, the other sports teams were never any good, so the budget for school sports always came to us. At other schools they usually focus more on the football team, but here it's all about baseball. Everyone shows up to the game to cheer us on!

The day of the home opener, I feel like an all-star, walking through the school. Every corner I turn I hear kids screaming my name. "Yo, Spence you ready to kick some tiger ass tonight?"

"You know it." I dab up at least fifteen kids, and each one looks up at me as if I'm some A-list celebrity. I try not to let it go to my head, but we all know it does.

A cute girl stops me in the hallway with her friends to tell me how excited they are to come see me play, "Hey Spencer, I'm so excited to see you play tonight, you're like totally, so cool." This is also around the time the incoming freshman girls start hitting on me. The guys and I usually play this game, to see how many girls would come up to us before the start of each game. I bet seven, but the others said over twenty. Until about this morning, I was winning, but with the game being tonight and my player poster being newly put up on the wall, I've already reached fifteen girls.

"Hope you girls enjoy," I pretend to wave to someone standing behind them so I wouldn't have to keep entertaining this conservation.

I head towards the open classroom, and to my surprise, Josie is already sitting in her seat. Usually, we walk together, especially on opener day, but I guess she got here early. I walk up beside her and kiss her on the cheek.

"Hey, beautiful."

"Hi Spence," she says a bit annoyingly.

"Are you coming to the game tonight?"

"Wouldn't miss it."

"Great!" I see Mrs. W walking into the class, so I give Josie a quick kiss and walk over to my seat.

Kayleigh is already sitting at our desk, and I notice her already reading the lab for today.

"Yo Satan, save some work for the rest of us."

"You know I would love to leave you some work, but someone has to prepare while the other one sucks his monstrous girlfriend's face." She mentions that last part with a little too much excitement.

"If I didn't know any better, I would think you're obsessed with her."

"Yeah right."

"It's alright Satan, you can admit it."

She turns and looks me up and down.

"Hold up, I feel very violated by that."

She rolls her eyes and brings her bag onto her lap. She rummages through her things and pulls out this small garbage bag and drops it right in front of me.

"This isn't going to explode, is it?" I very hesitantly go to reach for the bag but refrain from opening it till she answers me.

Kayleigh seems to enjoy my immediate discomfort because she takes a while to answer my question.

"No, Jackass, it's not gonna explode. But I'll remember that for next time."

"Oh, so you plan to make it a habit of getting me gifts? If that's the case I'm into sports, reading and the colour blue."

"You read?"

"Ouch. You don't have to act so surprised." I reach into the bag and pull out my lucky keychain. "Where the hell did you get this." I'm now holding the ripped-apart keychain in my left hand.

"The dumb thing fell in my car when you got out. You're lucky I didn't throw it away; the thing is hanging on by threads."

I bring the keychain into my chest as if it is my child. "This is my favourite keychain. My pops got it for me at my first-ever baseball game and I can't play a game without it." I take a deep breath, "I can't believe I didn't realize it was gone."

Kayleigh looks at me as if I'm crazy. "It's just a stupid keychain. Don't tell me you're one to have superstitions?"

"What's wrong with superstitions? At least I don't play god-awful music to impress my friends."

I felt proud of that one, I could really tell it ticked her off, but without saying anything in return she violently turns towards the front.

"Don't be like that Kayleigh. I was just joking around."
She doesn't answer me, and we don't talk for the remainder of
the class. *How did I take that too far?*

The bell finally rings and Kayleigh sprints out of the
classroom. I'm stuck putting all the equipment away and by the
time I'm finished, I can feel my girlfriend lingering behind me.
It makes the hairs on my neck stand up straight.

"What the hell Spencer?" I turn to her a bit puzzled, as
to say I have no clue what I did this time. "Why'd I see
Kayleigh give you a present."

I chuckle to myself. "It wasn't a present; she found my
lucky keychain and gave it back."

"Why'd she have your keychain? I'm not even allowed
to touch that piece of garbage."

"I don't know, maybe she saw it fall when I was
walking through the hallway." I avoid telling her that me and
Kayleigh volunteer together because that would just cause
more drama.

"Well, you didn't have to talk to her after she handed
it to you."

"I wasn't going to be rude and just grab it from her." I
sound aggravated because recently every conversation I have
with Josie has turned into a fight.

"You know how I feel about her."

"It's not like I was kissing her in the middle of the class."

"Oh, so now you're thinking about kissing her."

"You are just too much for me sometimes Josie, you know that." I grab my bag and walk out of class.

"Don't walk away from me."

"See you at the game Josie." I walk out without turning around as fast as I could because I do not want to say something that I'll regret.

...

** *Tonight, is the first home game for our Midrock Falls Knights, where they will be battling the West Valley Tigers. Now for the returning seniors for the Knights… Our captain playing shortstop…number 13… Spencer Brown. In center field, we have number 1 Reed Rivers. Behind the plate, we have number 7, Alec Rose. And on the mound, we have number 11, Tyler Burns.* **

The four of us run onto the field, as the crowd erupts into cheers. We normally have a lot of fans in the stands, but it looks like every kid form school is here, and that just pumps us up even more. Winning the last 3 championships boosted our attendance, especially for the season's first game. Since we have the home-field advantage the boys and I take our positions out into the field. Our first baseman is that transfer student, who ran onto the field before me, Colin, he is going to love the walk-up song we chose for him. He is technically a senior like me, but the announcer only calls the returning players for the first game. Anyways, we toss out a few grounders for a little practice then the ump starts the game.

We hope the first inning moves quick, three up, three down, but I don't think this will be easy.

Tyler started off strong, with a 0-2 pitch count. He then tried out some of the pitches we worked on in the summer and fumbled a bit. The count was then 3-2, so he went back to what was working. A clean pitch down the middle of the plate, gets the batter swinging. The crowd, cheers, as the ball makes its way around the horn.

I raise one finger in the air, and yell, "One out, boys."

Tyler's in his stance ready to throw the next ball but the batter is playing with his head a bit. He is staring him straight down, waiting for his next move. When Tyler lifts his leg, the batter chuckles and winks. I can tell by just looking at Ty, that he is freaked. The pitch goes in soft, and *bang*. The ball launches off the bat and comes straight towards my face. I wish I could say this next part is skill, but it's just a hell of a lot of luck. I lift my glove and hope for the best.

I fall back to the ground, the silence in the crowd is eerie. No one is saying a thing as I lie on the ground. I slowly lift my glove to show the white ball. Immediate cheers roar from the crowd, I cannot believe I just made that catch. Harrison, my third basemen is right by my side helping me up.

"Holy shit Spence, I knew you were good but seriously, you don't have to show us up this early on in the season."

I toss the ball to him and chuckle.

"There's plenty more where that came from buddy."

I dust my glove off and raise two fingers in the air. "Two outs now, two outs."

The next batter on the knights is the one we've been warned about. Jeremy "The Slinger" Holt, was the it guy all through summer training camp, he was by far the strongest, and the biggest. How this kid is in high school, I couldn't tell you. He's 6'4, built like a truck, has auburn hair, but has the face of a baby. From the back, this guy looks scary but from the front, he looks just like a giant teddy bear. He clearly has an issue with his baby face because he tried growing out his beard. Unfortunately, he can't grow one very well, so his whole face is patchy. It looks like he had sunflower seeds in his mouth and screwed up spiting them out.

Tyler obviously knows this guy's reputation because he starts off with a curveball, that Jeremy just misses. The next pitch to come in is off-speed, and the batter makes enough contact to send the ball to the outfield. The ball is falling right in between our right fielder and Reed, both guys are moving quickly, but the ball is going to be hard to catch. Just as the ball is about to land, Reed lunges forwards, 'Superman-style' to snag the baseball.

"Let's Go!" I scream.

The crowd goes crazy for that catch, and it's only the first half of the inning.

Reed jumps up and starts running back to the dugout. We all walk off the field with a little more energy because of the great start to the game but quickly realize that there is a lot more baseball to play.

Our turn at bat is equally as quick. The Tigers waste no time getting us out, so we head back into the field. We manage to have error after error after error, so the Tigers now lead 3-0. The rest of the game is more our speed. We hold the Knights to 3 runs going into the final inning. We are at the very bottom of our order with bases loaded, two outs, with the game on the line. To make matters worse it's Colin's turn to bat. I must give credit where credit is due, Colin's a solid player in practice, but these last few at bats he's been walking up to the plate with some huge ego and just keeps missing the ball. With the game on the line the poor kid looks absolutely petrified walking into the batter's box. I almost feel a little bad having played the theme song to Barbie every time he walked up to bat. *Almost.*

Reed looks over to me and cracks a smile every time he goes up to the plate though. So, I guess the rest of the guys enjoyed the joke. I start to feel a little remorseful but remember he messed with my superstition, and everyone knows never to mess with an athlete's superstition.

I turn my focus back onto the game to realize that the count is now 3-2. The best-case scenario, he gets on base and the top of our order comes up to bat. Worst-case scenario he completely fumbles and loses us the game. *Obviously, it wouldn't be all Colin's fault. I tend to get a little dramatic close to the end of our games.* The opposing team's pitcher is winding up and I can barely look. The ball is coming in hot and...

Kayleigh

"Oh my god," both Sadie and Kate are jumping up and down screaming as the ball travels over the fence. Cheers erupt all around us, as the scoreboard changes from 3-0 to 4-3 showing the winning score for the home team.

I usually hate coming to Alec and Reed's baseball games but since it was the first home game of the season, I figured I should at least make an appearance and not complain. I showed up late so Kate was telling me what was going on. We were being outplayed and couldn't get an out to save our lives. Kate isn't the best to give a play-by-play, but Sadie was too focused on the game. She only realized I was there 10 minutes later.

One thing about Sadie is that she loves anything her boyfriend does. When he first joined the team, she learnt every single rule. It's quite funny seeing her all stressed out about the game, it is almost as if she was on the field.

"I cannot believe they won!"

"Seriously, I was worried when I saw Colin going up to bat."

"Alec was saying he was good, but he really waited until the last minute to show us, but holy shit that hit was amazing. The baseball groupies will totally be all over him tonight."

"You too seriously need to get a grip." They both choose to ignore my comment and continue to rave about the game. We are waiting by the locker room for the boys to get out, we usually all go home together after the first game.

The only people waiting by the locker room are the girlfriends, the groupies, and the occasional parent. I'm the exception. I always get weird looks from the ones looking to suck up to the soulmate-free baseball players, but I've stopped caring what other people think.

Sadie turns to me, "How was your first day at the clinic? Did you meet the other volunteer?"

"Ugh, don't even get me started on the clinic. You won't even believe who it is. I swear I rather jump off a bridge them spend every week with him."

"Him?" Sadie and Kate look at each other with grins spreading across their faces. "You mean a potential soulmate?"

These girls get excited about anything and everything.

"Ha ha ha you guys are the funniest people ever. How many times do I have to tell you that I don't give a shit about my soulmate? I rather just go to the Bunker."

"Anyways, who's the "not" potential soulmate then."

Just as I'm about to break the news. The locker room door bursts open. Alec and Reed lead the pack as they come strolling over behind their girlfriends.

"You enjoy the game babe,"

"Hell yeah, I did Alec. The way you were catching every ball behind the plate made you look like the best player out there."

"Excuse me Sades, but I'm standing right here." Reed gives her his puppy dog eyes, and we all start to laugh.

"Shut up Rivers, you know I was better."

"Did you not see the diving catch I made?" A few seconds pass and Alec notices someone who can fix their problem. "Yo cap, come tell us who was better tonight."

My worst nightmare is happening. Spencer Brown has just come out of the locker room and is now walking over to us. His hair dripping with water, and he smells surprisingly good.

"What do you two dumb asses want now?"

"Rivers over here thinks he was better than me tonight, but my girl says otherwise."

"Well, I wouldn't want to go against what your girl says, so I'll give the title to you tonight."

Alec turns to Reed and gives him the bird. "Suck it, loser."

Spencer is laughing but before he walks away, he looks at me and smiles.

I try to play it off as if it did not happen, but my best friend doesn't miss a beat. She's Nancy Drew when it comes to this shit.

"No fucking way Kayls! Spencer is the other senior at the clinic." She is practically yelling this in the hallway.

"Shut up Sadie, I don't need you waking the dead."

Both she and Kate look at each other as if they share one brain cell. "What if he's your soulmate? I can picture it now. Kayleigh Harris and Spencer Browns... SOULMATES."

They must think they're the world's biggest comedians because all four of them are laughing to themselves.

"All right, all right, get it out of your system now, because I can promise you that Spencer Brown, the boy who is head over heels for my arch nemesis is not my soulmate."

"We know Kayls, we just like seeing you squirm."

"Well did it work?"

"You should've seen your face little Kay. It was a whole other shade of red."

I stick my finger in the air. "Fuck you all. Spencer Brown is not, and will never be my soulmate."

Chapter 10
SPENCER

The high after the first home game will last forever, especially when we win. Usually, the seniors plan this massive ragger, near the beach and this year is no different, we have been planning this for weeks now. The music is already blasting through the air as my girl, and I pull up. I run around to Josie's side of the car to open her door — *because I'm just a gentleman like that*. She grabs my hand and slowly makes her way out. Josie looks mighty fine tonight, with her beach blond hair pulled back into a slick ponytail, with the smallest burgundy dress she could get her hands on. This dress is hugging her in all the right places, from her chest to her legs, my girl looks like a runway model. I'm not the only one who thinks so, because a group of guys started shuffling their way towards us and they look hungry.

The leader of the bro pack is Colin, since he hit the game winning ball, he's ego shot through the roof. He has this new cockiness to him, but it'll die down eventually, anyways he makes his way to me and taps me on the shoulder. "Hey, Cap. You better watch out tonight." He rubs his hands together and looks directly at Josie's chest.

"Settle down there Colin, I could have you running laps till the start of next season."

"All jokes Cap. But seriously your girl would look so good with me." He keeps eyeing Josie, which makes her grin just a little.

I take a step closer to him, but Josie grabs my arm.

"You should start looking for your actual soulmate, instead of chasing mine. Your time is running out, so you better get on it buddy."

Colin raises his hands in the air as if to say, he's innocent. Me and Josie walk past them hand in hand leaving them to stand in their drool. I'm still heated from the reaction, Josie gave. I try not to overthink it, but something was just off. I try my best to play it off, so I look back with a devilish smile and the boys start to howler. The guys know I can take a joke, so long as they can take one in return, but I quickly mouth to Colin that if he tries that again he will be running laps until his feet fall off. He acknowledges and walks off.

Usually at these parties, I stay close to Josie, because even though I am the captain of the most important sports team at Midrock Falls High, parties just aren't my thing. Josie is the social butterfly between the two of us and if it were my choice, we would be at home doing literally anything else. But I put on a brave face and come to these things because it makes my girlfriend happy. We've been here for about an hour or so and I've already lost her. She went off with a few of her friends as soon as we got here, and she hasn't come back. Don't get me wrong she can do whatever she wants, but my social battery has reached its limit and I'm starting to lose patience for the continuous cycle of groupies coming up to me. When I thought things couldn't get any worse, I see Satan walk in with her friends.

Alec and Reed must have spotted me because the group is slowly making their way towards the corner, I am standing in. I noticed that the two small girls next to them are whispering to each other and giggling. If I was more self-conscious that would hurt my ego, but whatever they had said got a reaction out of Kayleigh, so maybe the three of us could get along just fine.

"Look who finally decided to show up." I throw my arm around Reed's shoulder.

"It looks to me like you were doing just fine on your own." Reed glances towards the blonde I was trying to get rid of before they came over.

"Where's the worst half of you anyways Cap." This gets a smile out of Kayleigh, and I've never noticed how nice her smile is.

I can't help but snort, most of the boy's love Josie, but not these two, I'm assuming they are team Kayleigh for whatever reason they hate each other. "She went off with her minions a little while ago, haven't seen her since."

"She's probably coming up with the best way to make the new freshmen her slaves, or to teach dogs to scare off anyone with a poor sense of style."

"Wow, Satan I was expecting something more clever. She's already figured both those things out." She looks at me with a sarcastic grin before the girl standing next to Reed speaks up.

"Satan?" she laughs. "What the fuck type of nickname is that."

"Honestly bro, how does she let you call her that, when I can't even call her little Kay." Kayleigh's reflexes are on point, because before Alec could even finish his sentence, he's rubbing his arm from where Kayleigh had just slapped him.

"Alec, I swear to god, if you keep calling me that my fist will go so far up your ass your kids will feel it." I'm practically rolling on the floor at this point.

"Little Kay? I'm gonna save that one for a rainy day."

"You better watch it Brown or the next time I see your aunt, will be at your funeral."

"Wow settle down," Even with the threat I can't stop myself from laughing. It is so easy to get under her skin, it's my new favourite game.

I've figured out that the girl standing with Alec is Kayleigh's best friend Sadie, the two of them are inseparable except for when Sadie whispers something to her and kisses her on the cheek. She grabs Alec's hand, and they walk towards the kitchen together. That just leaves me, Kayleigh, Reed and Kate. *Who I just realized was Alec's twin.*

Reed and I go back and forth discussing the game for a few minutes until I overhear the two girls talking. Kayleigh is begging Kate not to leave her but doesn't seem to convince her. Sadie and Alec are watching us from a distance and motion for Reed and Kate to join them. Kayleigh tries to follow but Rivers insists she stays. I'm usually the one in her position where I was dragged somewhere that I don't want to be.

Knowing that she absolutely hates the idea of being alone with me, I play along and urge her to stay.

"Come on little Kay you know I don't bite." Her big blue eyes are staring me down. I could feel the daggers stabbing into me. Although she is much shorter than me, by the way she is looking through me I can feel myself getting smaller and smaller. I feel a shiver crawl up my spine.

"I'm actually going to kill those guys." She huffs out a breath.

"Please don't, I need them for the rest of the season."

This girl is not giving me the time of day. It's usually easy for me to talk to a girl because they hang onto every word that comes out of my mouth, but this one is a challenge. *Have I mentioned I love challenges?*

"You want something to drink Satan? Your cup looks kinda empty."

She looks down at her red solo cup and lifts her shoulders, "As long as I pour the thing. I don't trust you; you might poison me."

We walk over to the kitchen, and she grabs the tequila bottle. "I never deemed you for a tequila girl."

"You know very little about me Jackass." She downs the drink in a fraction of a second. She reaches to poor another, but I put my cup out in front of her. "What do you think you're doing?"

"You took one, so I get one. That's how it works Satan." She doesn't deny me the request, so we each do two more shots before I tap out and grab some water.

I toss a bottle towards her. "Here, drink this." She grabs the water with no second thought. "Can't lose my clinic and bio partner in one day. I can't do all the work by myself."

What almost seems like a genuine smile from Satan turns into an insult. "Can you do anything without me Jackass?"

If I didn't know any better, someone might think she likes me. But I know not to comment on that unless I want to lose some body part tonight.

Spending most of the night with Kayleigh is not entirely bad. She's one of the only people I know who can take a joke just as much as she can dish 'em out. We have gone back and forth all night insulting each other, and I've loved every minute of it. At one point during the night, we even walked out onto the beach, but when she started to get too cold, we made our way back in the beach house and Kayleigh's demeanour changes drastically. I ask her what's wrong, but she is too focused on something happening behind my head. I look to see what has caught her gaze, but she tries to distract me from it.

"What's the matter with you?"

"Nothing." She's quieter than usual, and I'm a little off edge with it. She grabs my arm to avoid me from turning around.

"Seriously Satan, what is wrong with you, let go of my arm."

"No Jackass, let's go play a round of beer pong, Sadie and Alec are there right now." I almost give in to the suggestion but as soon as she lets go, I turn around.

My heart sinks to my stomach as I see Josie and Colin walking out of a room together. Her hair is not as slicked back as before and the grin on Colin's face is magnetic. Josie's eyes meet with mine and she looks like the devil.

She is running towards me when I notice that Kayleigh has already marched off towards Sadie and Alec, who are watching with concerned eyes from afar.

"Are you fucking serious right now Spencer? What are you doing with that bitch." I'm too stunned to speak.

"Hello?" she is waving her hand in front of my face before I snap out of whatever trance I was just in.

"I- I don't know what you're talking about." *Seriously Spencer that's what you come up with. You see your girlfriend coming out of a room with some other guy and that's what you say.*

Josie's voice goes softer, "Babe, you know how much I don't like her, why would you do that to me."

"Do that to you? Weren't you the one who just walked out of that room with Colin?"

She flattens out her dress and looks back at Colin. "Oh, that? That was nothing, babe, I was just showing him where the bathroom was, it's not a big deal."

My face is still frozen in place, and I no longer know how to react. "No big deal?"

"Come on Cap, you know I would never do that to you." Colin is now standing behind Josie, but she turns around and pushes him back. He nods and walks off agitated.

She plays the victim card well because, without a second thought, she has tears running down her face. "Spencer, do you really not trust me, that you think I would cheat on you?"

She whimpers until I tell her I trust her completely. "Good." With that being said she is back to being completely fine, with no sign of tears. "I'm getting really tired babe would you mind driving me home?"

"Actually, I think I'm going to stay for a little while longer, I promised Alec I would play a round of beer pong."

I don't think that was the response Josie was looking for because she seems a little taken aback. "Oh, okay sweetie, I'll just catch a ride with one of the girls."

"Sounds good babe. Love you." She just nods towards me and walks out the front door.

When Josie leaves, I make my way to Alec, Sadie and Kayleigh who are still standing by the beer pong table observing what had just occurred. Without missing a beat, I turn to Kayleigh.

"You ready to kick some ass." She seems surprised and genuinely concerned but I don't let any of them console me for what just happened. Instead, I pick up the ping pong ball and start playing.

Chapter 11
Kayleigh

So far, I have cleaned the back room, organized the front desk, and labelled all the prescriptions. I have already been volunteering here for a few weeks and I have yet to learn anything about helping the animals.

It has mostly just been me here with the receptionist and Dr. Patty. Spencer came in for a couple of minutes the Thursday after the party but quickly left after speaking to his aunt. He had looked my way once, and I tried waving, but he ducked his head and walked straight out the door. It took a lot of convincing, but I was eventually able to get Lianne to tell me why Spencer hadn't come in during our scheduled shifts.

She mentioned that he still comes in for the required time, just at another time during the week. She overheard him saying to Dr. Patty that his girlfriend threw a fit about some girl, and instead of arguing, he insisted that for the next few weeks, he would just come in another time.

As much as it pains me to admit, having Spencer around makes the job a lot less boring. Being able to throw insults at each other, often lifts my spirits. It's no surprise to me that the reincarnation of the devil herself has required her boyfriend to stay as far away from me as possible. When Lianne said it was about another girl, I immediately assumed that girl was me. Even during our last biology class, Spencer would only talk to me when we were working on our lab. He has also stopped saying hi to me when I would walk into class.

I was already sitting at our shared desk when he walked in with Josie. I lifted my hand to say hi, but Josie tugged on his arm and his expression was stone cold. When he came to sit down, I tried egging him on, but he just motioned to Josie, and I got the message.

I spoke to Dr. Patty before the start of my shift to see if I could do a few extra hours at the end of the day because next week I wouldn't be able to come in. She agreed almost immediately and told me that since I needed to stay later that I could just close the shop. It's a huge pat on the back because that means she trusts me with a set of keys.

It's been a few minutes since both Lianne and Dr. Patty have left the clinic, I'm in the back cleaning up the operation room when I hear the chimes of the door opening. I could have sworn that I turned over the sign to say we were closed so my first instinct was to hide in the corner because some intruder just walked in, but my parents didn't raise a coward. I picked up the closest thing I could find, which was the lid of a cookie jar and proceeded to confront whoever just walked through the door.

I slowly make my way towards the front of the clinic and as I'm about to smash the lid onto the unsuspecting intruder, I freeze.

"Jesus Christ Satan. What are you doing with a fucking cookie jar lid?" He takes out his earphones and grabs the glass lid out of my hands.

"I thought you were an intruder. Lianne never said you come in late on Thursdays. She just said you come another time."

Spencer is chuckling as he puts the glass lid on the counter. "You're telling me, that you thought I was robbing the place and decided to use a lid as your weapon of choice?"

I slap him on the shoulder as I make my way back to the operating room. "You're a jackass you know that?"

"And you were asking Lianne about me. Should I be flattered?"

"Fuck off." I turn around to see that he has a smug look on his face. *This is the kind of interaction I've missed.* His cockiness affects me in a certain way, and I could not get it out of my head.

I cannot believe he comes late every Thursday just to avoid me. I imagine it's because Josie is just a jealous piece of shit but, come on, you would think the poor guy has a mind of his own.

When Spencer makes his way to the room, I'm already cleaning, I can't help but notice the way he looks. His shoulders are hunched, and he looks physically exhausted. "Is practice getting the best of you nowadays?"

He shrugs but does not respond. "Not even a sarcastic comeback? I'm shocked. You must be really tired."

I can tell something is off with Spencer; he is usually quick on his feet and ready with some sort of comeback but today he just seems deflated. I don't try to pry anything else out of him for a good half hour, but the silence is eating away at me. When I go towards the stereo to turn on the music I queued up from before he got here, he starts to talk.

"I'm not a bad person you know." I looked at him a bit confused as to where that comment came from but refrain from saying anything.

"Just as I was about to play some killer music too," I whisper to myself. I see him trying to figure out what to say next. He has this look on his face, I can practically see the wheels spinning in his head. I give him a couple of seconds to figure out his thoughts.

"You haven't said much to me after what happened at the party a few weeks back."

"It's not like you gave me many chances, Jackass," I say facing him. "You've sort of been MIA."

He doesn't respond so I take the opportunity to ask him what I've been wanting to ask him since he left the party.

"How are things with the devil?" He looks up at me but tries to hide the small grin appearing on his face.

"Josie's good, she felt bad for what happened at the party, so she came over the next day to make it up to me."

I simply nod, because I don't want him to start going into all the gory details of their adventures. But he is a little dense, so he doesn't get the memo.

"She showed up at my house wearing my baseball jersey. Just my baseball jersey." He has the nerve to wink at me. *Wink at me, is this guy nuts?* You can see him reminiscing the events in his head while he tries to figure out what the next detail he wants to share. "My parents weren't home, so we spent time in every room possible."

I think I'm going to vomit.

Just as he was about to tell me how he got her off for the second time I interjected. "As much as I would love to hear all the ways you two had a memorable time, I'd rather jump off the roof into a pile of shit, and then burn myself alive."

His face turns a slight shade of pink, "My bad."

"Anyways, instead of reciting a play-by-play, why don't you pick up the broom and help me sweep."

Without hesitation, he goes to get the broom, he lifts two fingers towards his head and says, "Right away captain."

This makes my stomach fill with butterflies, I can't tell if I love or hate this feeling, but Spencer Brown's ego is far too big for him to know his actions affect me in any way. When he passes by the stereo he turns the volume up, so we can both hear the music. I set it up so that when the playlist ends, we should be done. A good hour and a half passes until the very last song finishes. We are both humming to the music when it stops. It turns out we work well together when we aren't arguing. We have cleaned every inch of this place in a very short amount of time. We are both gathering our things when I pull out my phone to see three missed texts from my dad and a missed call.

Dad: *Hey sweetie. How's it going?*

Dad: *What time do you need me to come and get you?*

I am getting ready for bed if I don't hear back from you.

Dad: *Text me when you get this, please. I am in bed.*

Missed call: Dad.

Me: *Just finished up.*

Me: *Have you already gone to bed?*

A few minutes pass and no response. "Great," I say under my breath. Spencer just finished locking up the door when he walked up beside me.

"Everything alright?"

"Yeah, all's good. My ride just decided to fall asleep so I'm just going to walk home."

"It's almost midnight. There's no way I'm letting you walk home alone."

I would usually argue about how I'm a grown woman who can make her way home by herself, but it's been a long day and I don't really feel like getting home at 1 in the morning.

"We'll call it even since you drove me home the first time." The two of us walk towards his car, it is the only one sitting in the dark parking lot adjacent to the clinic. The streetlights hanging above us are flickering, and it gives the cool night air an ominous feeling. Maybe taking Spence up on this offer was a good move.

Instinctively I go to grab the aux to play my music but before I can plug my phone in, Spencer looks over to me. "What do you think you're doing? My car, my music." I throw my hands up in the air as if to say, all yours. He plugs his phone in, and begins to flip through his playlists until he stumbles upon one that puts a smile on his face.

Better than Revenge by Taylor Swift starts playing in the car. I look at him with shock in my eyes. "Why were you giving me so much shit, if you like T. Swift?" He begins pulling out of the parking lot and looks over at me.

"Who in their right mind doesn't like a little T. Swift?"

For the entire drive home, we both equally chant our way through three Taylor Swifts songs. I can't help but let out a sigh when I see him pulling down my street. He parks the car in front of my house, I hesitate before leaving the car. I'm not sure why, but I can't bring myself to open the door. I sit there for a couple of seconds and just as I reach for the door handle, he clears his throat.

"That was fun. I haven't let myself sing to a song like that in such a long time." He is beaming with delight.

"I've never seen someone like you, know the full chorus to Paper Rings."

He flashes a smile at me, and I feel a flutter from within. *WTF was that?* "What do you mean someone like me?"

"You know… a jackass." I'm looking into his eyes waiting for his comeback but nothing, all I see is a change in his demeanor, something is off, his eyes go a little dark and I fight the urge to question him about it but who's to say it's any of my business? I don't want to overstep.

"Anyways, thanks for the ride."

I am still stuck in my seat, unable to move. Something in me still doesn't allow me to get out of the car, so instead, I let go of the door and turn my whole body to face him.

"Ok," I grunt, "What is going on with you."

He looks a bit frazzled. I don't think he was expecting me to question him. "Seriously, what's with the look."

"What look?" He seems to not know what I'm talking about, so I push further.

"The look you're giving me right now. It's a mix of, I have something to tell you, but I don't know how to say it."

"Satan chill, I'm not giving you any look." I know he's lying because his face turned another shade of red, the poor guy is embarrassed now.

"Fine then, I'll say what I've been thinking this entire time." He looks a bit on edge, I don't know what he thinks I'm going to say but he is all ears. "I don't believe you when you said everything was good with Josie."

He doesn't agree or disagree, so I take it as an invitation to push further. "You seemed very closed off ever since that party, and don't get me wrong I love the quiet, but I did miss the occasional competition between the two of us. It's not as fun when I don't have someone to constantly make fun of."

"Wow little Kay, I don't know if I should feel touched or offended." *Is he seriously making jokes right now?* I choose to brush off the little Kay comment for now, but I'll remember it for next time.

"Whatever, Jackass, I was genuinely trying to be nice." I reach for the door handle and push it open but before I step out of the door, I quickly turn around and grab his phone from the cup holder.

"What are you-." I cut him off by putting my hand in the air.

"I'm putting my number into your phone so you can text me when you get home, or if you decide you need to talk to someone, about whatever the fuck is going on."

Before he can comment on my actions, I jump out of the car and quickly walk towards my front door without turning around.

The voice inside my head is quickly questioning what I had just done. *Why would I give him my number? Kayleigh what the hell was that?* I walk into my house and head for my room. After I put my bags down and change into my pajamas, I hear a message pop up on my phone.

Unknown number: I'm *home!*

I go to put my phone down but hear another notification.

Unknown number: *took me a while to find your* contact.

Unknown number: *nice touch putting your name as Satan! But I'm debating changing it to Little Kay.*

Me: *don't even think about it Jackass.*

That's my reminder to add his contact info as Jackass. I edit his contact and take a screenshot to send over.

> Jackass: *Nice. I get a nickname in ur phone.*
>
> Me: *Don't flatter ur-self 2 much.*
>
> Jackass: *no way ur someone who types the number 2 instead of too.*
>
> Me: *does it make you angry?*
>
> Jackass: *if I say it does will u continue to do it?*
>
> Me: *maybe :)*
>
> Jackass: *fine then I don't mind it at all*
>
> Me: *perf! see u 2morrow*

I see the grey bubbles pop up insinuating that he is about to type back but then they disappear, so I go and finish getting ready for bed, I plug my phone into the wall and notice one unread message, and it is from him.

> Jackass: *gn :)*

I am fully aware of the smile that crosses my face when I see the text from him. I shut my phone off and pray I'm not starting to fall for this guy. But as I lay in bed awake thinking about him, how his muscles were perfectly outlined by his white dry-fit t-shirt today, and how he smelt amazing whenever he walked past me in the clinic, my eyes shoot open, and I let out a giant sigh.

"Oh shit."

Chapter 12

Kayleigh

I wake up covered in sweat and my heart is racing, I just had the worst dream of my life. 'I had fallen head over heels for Spencer, and to prove my love I had to go up against Josie in some sort of battle. Spencer then couldn't decide between the two of us and just as he was about to make his decision I woke up.' I roll over on my bed and plant my face into my pillow.

The muffled screams fill my room and I hear my parents running up the stairs.

"Honey, what's the matter? We heard screaming." My parents are both panting when they make it to my room.

I roll back over, "Just had the worst dream possible!"

"You scared us their sweetie, next time don't scream so loud." They both walk back out of my room as I sarcastically mouth the words 'Love you too.'

The newly kicked-in adrenaline allows me to get ready in record time, I'm fully dressed and down the stairs before Sadie even walks into the house.

"Good morning, Harris family! How is everyone doing on this fine morning?" This girl always has a spring to her step, but she comes to an abrupt halt when she notices me all put together and eager to leave.

"My god, Kayls, I almost didn't recognize you." She slaps her hand to her mouth to act surprised, I turn her around and push her out the front door.

"Come on, I just walked in, and the breakfast your parents made smells amazing."

"Sades, I have so much to tell you." Her eyes light up with anticipation and she quickly forgets about the food on the table.

...

I wait until everyone gets into the car before I start spilling my newfound dilemma. Sadie is eager to find out what news I'm so desperately trying to share, she sticks her head out of the sunroof to get her boyfriend to move quicker.

"Hurry up babe! Kayls has some big news to tell us." Alec doesn't get the message the first time, so Sadie sticks her head out again, "I swear to god Alec Rose if you don't move your ass, I'm leaving you here."

Kate and I look at each other before laughing uncontrollably. Have I mentioned that she can sometimes, *(always),* be a little too dramatic?

When Alec finally reaches the car, Sadie jumps in her seat with anticipation.

"Relax, drama queen, you're going to fall out of your seat if you keep jumping like that."

Sadie is not one to play around when gossip is involved, she looks back at Alec, which quiets him quickly. She then looks over to me, and I can't lie I got kind of scared.

"Ok spill it, Kayleigh. You've made me wait forever for this news."

"It's been five minutes Sades, you violated every road sign there was getting here."

She doesn't even comment on the jab at her driving skills, she's just waiting for me to spill the tea.

"Ok fine. Last night I stayed late at the vet clinic and-." I pause to ensure anticipation.

"And what?" Barks out, Sadie.

I quickly mumble the rest of my sentence. "-and I think a part of me is interested in Spencer."

"What did you just say." Alec looks at me with open eyes, and Sadie and Kate sit there stunned.

"I said, 'I think a part of me is interested in Spencer' like obviously he's annoying and a jackass but in an endearing type of way." The whole car goes silent. Not a single person is saying anything, and I feel super out of place right now.

"Come on guys say something for Christ's sake."

Sadie looks at Kate in the rearview mirror and they both shriek.

"I told you, Sadie, I knew the two of them would eventually get together."

"Oh my god Kayls this is amazing!"

"Hold up, little Kay likes Spence?"

"Get with the program babe, obviously she does."

"Hold up, I don't even know if I like him. I just had a strange dream about him, where I was fighting Josie for him, and I get the occasional butterfly feeling when he passes me in the clinic.

Sadie looks too stunned to speak but manages to muster up a response, "So you're telling me you had a dream about the hottest guy in school and you still aren't sure if you like him?" I nod my head.

"Excuse me, Sadie, but I thought I was the hottest guy in school." Sadie raises her hand to silence Alec. The poor guy looks devastated even though he knows she didn't mean it like that.

The rest of the car ride consists of my friends trying to convince me I have feelings for Spencer. Obviously, he has the looks, and he can handle my sarcasm, but he is super in love with Josie, so he must have some red flags underneath the surface. Sadie was trying to convince me that it was the perfect opportunity to fuck her over in terms of soulmates, but then that would suggest that Spencer is my soulmate and not hers. I don't want to screw Spencer over if I'm not his soulmate. Plus, I would have to be a shallow person to mess with a soulmate pairing for shits and giggles. My first class of the day is the biology lab, so the group collectively decided to walk me to class and hype me up before I start walking in.

I don't know what's wrong with me, usually I'm never nervous walking into a class but today, I'm shitting myself. Luckily, I get there before Spencer does, it gives me time to plan out what I'm going to say. I quickly realize everything I had come up with so far is garbage, so when I see him walk into class, I panic a little, however, it subsides when I notice the rat at his heels. Her golden hair sways back and forth as she follows him to her seat. I keep down the build-up of vomit in my throat. The bell's about to ring so Spencer finally makes his way over to our table which is in the front of the classroom and out of earshot of Josie's.

He doesn't even look my way and mostly whispers when he speaks to me. The first thing he says is "Hey, Satan," but nothing follows. I would normally think nothing of it, but it affects me today. I feel a nerve in my body twitch a little when he doesn't give me the time of day.

In my most sarcastic tone, I try to pull more out of him. "Wow Jackass, not even going to look at me? I see how it is."

His lips started to pull into a grin when Mrs. W waltzed into the class. My delusion is thinking that I still have a chance, but whenever I get a reaction out of him, it makes me happy. Today's lesson could not be better for me. The teacher assigns half the class to do part A of the experiment outside in the courtyard, and the rest of the class is assigned to part B, which is to be done inside. Spencer and I are staying inside, while Josie and his friends are outside. When we begin our part of the project, I can't help but smile to myself. However, I'm not as slick as I thought, because Spencer notices right away.

"You can't seriously be this happy looking at the anatomy of a leaf cell."

I snap back into focus when I hear his voice, "Oh sorry, my head was somewhere else." *Nice cover, dumbass.* "Anyways let's get back to it."

"No need Satan, I've already finished our part." I look at him in absolute shock, how did he finish this so quickly?

"No fucking way." He laughs at my immediate surprise.

"I told you; bio is my favourite subject." He's already packing up his bag before I even comprehend that he finished the work. We've been working together since the start of the year, so I don't even bother looking over what he did. Spencer calls over Mrs. W with a wave of his hand. "Mrs. we've already finished our part."

She looks pleased with the work that Spencer hands her. "I told you both at the start of this semester, that you two would be a good paring. You guys may be dismissed, have a good rest of the week."

I quickly pack up my things and catch up to Spencer who has already left the class.

"You seriously did not just leave me in the class."

"Sorry, little Kay, your legs are just too small to keep up."

"You have called me little Kay twice now with no repercussion, you better watch your back Jackass."

"Oh no, I'm so scared."

"Don't underestimate me. I may be small but I'm feisty."

"Oh yeah?" He halts in the middle of the hallway facing me now. I stop to look at him directly in his eyes. "Yeah." We both stay silent for a few seconds before he turns back towards the exit.

"What are your plans now, since you finished our paper within 30 minutes of the class starting?"

"I was going to head on out, my last class of the day got cancelled. It's the first day I get to go home and relax."

"Oh." I sound way more disappointed than I was anticipating but luckily, he doesn't notice.

"What are you going to do?"

"I have to wait for Sadie to finish her class, she's my ride home." He stays silent in front of me for a few seconds, before saying what he has been contemplating in his head. I could tell that major internal negotiations were happening, but he finally figured out a solution.

"I can give you a lift if you want. I mean, I did drive you home already and it's not like it's out of the way." My whole body defies me; my stomach has butterflies, and my face is flushed.

"Seriously? I would appreciate it if you could." He doesn't immediately take away the offer when I agree, so we head out towards his car. We both walked the long way to get to the parking lot because Spencer wanted to avoid where the other group of kids were, so we didn't pass Josie. I don't complain, I could go without seeing her face ever again.

When we reach the car, we start playing the music from where we left off. It's as if no time has passed, and we both start singing the lyrics.

A note of disappointment crosses my face when I see the familiar driveway come into view. We barely spoke during this car ride, as we were singing the entire time. Spencer puts the car in park and waits for me to get out of the car.

"Thanks for the lift, Jackass, I owe you one." I hesitate to get out, as I am waiting to see if Spencer will say anything back. If I'm the only one catching feelings, I rather bite it in the ass now than waste my energy trying. When he doesn't open his mouth, I start to reach for the door handle.

"Satan, hold on a second." I'm not even facing him at this point, and that's a good thing because my face defies me once again, my smile is no longer containable. I wait until I have full control of my face before turning back to face him.

"I wanted to say sorry about being distant, Josie and I had this huge fight and it's just easier to avoid you." I can't tell if I'm hurt that he needed to avoid me, or if I should be happy that he and Josie are fighting. I don't push for details on what the fight was about, having known Josie, it was probably some stupid shit that was her fault anyways.

"Don't worry about it. It's not like I'm waiting for you by the phone all day." I think I hit a nerve because his face darkens at the sound of my voice.

"No yeah, you're right. You probably didn't even notice." *What the hell is wrong with you? Of course, you noticed.* This stupid voice in my head will not give me a break.

I'm looking at his eyes now, "Anything else you wanted to say?" His eyes say yes but his lips say no. I lean towards him a little bit more and hear the hitch of his breath. I don't know where any of this is coming from, but if we both just lean in a little more our lips would be touching. My body defies me for the third time today, and I slowly back away from him. I grunt a little bit before opening the car door.

I gently close it and motion for him to open the window. He rolls the window of his car down and waits for me to speak. "Thanks again for the ride, I still owe you one."

"No problem. That's what friends are for." *Damn.* That's like a knife through the chest. I'm walking away from the car but quickly turn around to tell him that instead of avoiding me he could just text me. I can't tell if I've gone too far yet, but the smile that lights up his face as he pulls away tells me I have so much more room to work with.

Chapter 13
SPENCER

What is wrong with me? I have the most beautiful girl lying in my bed willing to do absolutely anything, and I can barely give her the time of day. I can tell that Josie has been putting in a lot more effort since the party, but things have felt different with her. I no longer feel excited to see her, and whenever I get a text and her name pops up on the screen, I roll my eyes. She's started to catch on that I'm no longer giving her the attention she wants because she looks at me with questions in her eyes.

"What's the matter, babe?" she has her head leaning against my bare chest, angled up to look at me. "You seem to be somewhere else."

I sit up so my back is leaning against the headboard, and I move Josie so that she is straddling my legs. I place my hands around her waist and we both look at each other. "Sorry sweetie, I've just had a lot on my mind." *How am I supposed to tell her that the thing on my mind is her ex-best friend?* Here's the answer... You don't. I take a while to muster up a response, it's a good thing that Josie does not truly care what other people are thinking because she drops the subject rather quickly.

She works her way up my chest until I can feel her lips move across my jaw. She nudges her head into the crook of my neck and spends a few minutes giving all her undivided attention to that one spot that she knows drives me crazy. I give in to her temptation and lift the bottom of her chin so our lips can finally meet. Within seconds her tongue grazes the part between my lips, and I give her full access to my mouth. She's hungry for this, our kiss is very sloppy, but neither one of us seems to care. She grinds against me to deepen the kiss, as her hands travel up and down my chest, outlining every muscle she meets.

Josie is waiting for me to do more; she slithers down my body until she sits comfortably between my legs. She continues exploring my bare body navigating her way through the dips in my abs when she meets the waistband of my grey sweats, she does not hesitate to yank them down, revealing that I am indeed going commando. I notice her eyes light up and a slight smile forms on her lips, she reaches out for my bare body and wraps her hand around the base of my shaft. When she squeezes me, I let out a groan letting her know that that's what I want. She looks at me with her doe eyes and licks her bottom lip. Without a second thought, she has her lips wrapped around the tip of me, and I grab the side of the comforter to steady myself. "That's it, babe. That feels so good." When she hears the satisfaction in my voice, she quickens her pace. Rubbing and sucking simultaneously almost knocking me over the edge, I do my best to hold on a little longer because I can't get enough of this feeling. "Josie," I pant, "I'm almost there." A few more seconds, and I explode in her mouth. I shiver from the release and relax my entire body. She hops up and goes to the bathroom to clean herself up.

"You feel a little bit better now babe?" She is crawling her way back into my bed. I nod my head in agreement.

Recently I have noticed that whenever the two of us are together we rarely do things to pleasure us both at the same time. Either she's going down on me, or I'm going down on her. I must've hit my head during practice because what teenage boy in their right mind complains about getting too many BJs? It's the same routine with Josie and I'm starting to wonder if it's something I did wrong. Whenever I bring it up to her, she always pushes the topic aside and distracts me in the only have she knows how.

We've been lying in bed for the past few minutes in complete silence. She's resting on my chest again and I'm brushing my fingers through her silky-smooth hair. "You know," she looks up at me, "things have been very different between us lately." She repositions herself and she starts tracing my abs with her fingers. "What do you mean Spence?"

"Just, we don't seem to be having as much fun together as we used to, you know."

"Do you need me to go down on you again?" She sounds agitated but has a sly smile on her face. "Because I will gladly go for round two if you need me to."

"It's not just that though Josie, just everything seems so forced."

"Come on babe, everyone has their rough patches. Let me make you feel better again."

It's like a routine with this girl, before I can even protest her into having an actual conversation, she has already positioned herself the same way she was before and dives right in for round two.

Rather than enjoying the view of my beautiful girlfriend, sucking me off, I can't help but notice that my mind is somewhere else. I'm thinking about those sarcastic blue eyes, rolling every time I try to speak. I'm thinking about the girl who barely gives me the time of day. I'm thinking about how her hair falls perfectly over her shoulder, and how she always has new paintings on the jeans she wears to school. I'm thinking about how the two of us can joke around without it ending in an argument. I'm just thinking about her.

I'm thinking about the one girl who I shouldn't be thinking about. My soulmate is right in front of me trying to make me feel better, and all I'm doing is confusing myself. The 4th is coming quickly, and Josie has already told me that we are a perfect match. Her father has records of all the soulmates so why do I feel so connected to Kayleigh? Things might have been too comfortable with Josie lately but that doesn't mean I should throw it all away because some girl is more exciting, right? It's not like I can avoid her either, next time I see her, I'll tell her what I've been thinking, and then she can laugh in my face, and all could be forgotten.

Nice work Spence, the voice in my head sounds pleased with itself, *no chance that plan fails.*

Chapter 14
Kayleigh

It's been a couple of days since I last saw Spencer Brown, and almost every waking minute, I have been thinking only of him; of his eyes, his hair, the way his muscles contract when he does his work. I'm turning into this girl who obsesses over boys, and it is freaking me the fuck out.

I occasionally catch myself staring at my phone waiting for a notification hoping it will be from him. When I woke up this morning, I had several notifications from my friends asking me, if I was still hanging out with them later that night.

Sades: *Kayls ur still good for tnt right?*

Sades: *I wouldn't blame u if u bail.*

Sades: *Thursday is when you see spency ;)*

Kate: *Omg is Kayleigh bailing on us for a boy??!!*

Sades: *I wouldn't be mad if she did.*

Sades: *As long as we get all the details.*

Reed: *For fuck's sake Sadie it's not even 8 am yet.*

Alec: *I agree with Reed babes it's too early for this.*

Sades: *Both of u shut up <3*

Alec: *Luv u too*

Reed: *She isn't seriously going to bail?*

Kate: *You jealous or smt lmao.*

Reed: *Yes sweetie, I am super jealous because Kayleigh wants to ride his dick.*

Sades: *Must u use those words.*

Reed: *WHAT? if Alec said it, you'd be fine with it.*

Alec: *Don't drag me into this asshole.*

Me: *Good morning to u too guys!*

Me: *And no, I will not be bailing on any of u.*

Sades: *R u serious??*

Me: *You've known me long enough.*

Me: *I wouldn't bail on my friends for some boy toy.*

Kate: *Even if the boy toy was drool-worthy?*

Reed: *Watch it missy!!*

Kate: *lmfao I'll make it up to you ;)*

Sades: *Ok enough of whatever that was.*

                          Me: *I'm not bailing end of discussion*

                            Me: *See y'all soon <3*

I throw my phone onto the bed so I can start getting ready for the day. I throw on my typical school outfit, which consists of a baggy band tee and my custom-designed jeans. I'm starting to run out of good drawing space. I should seriously invest in a new pair.

Getting to school was the same as usual, we drove in all together meeting Reed near our parking spot. We all walk hand in hand until I notice the flyers on the school wall.

'All seniors: soulmate selection day is coming quickly. Mark your calendars for May 4th. Only four months to go!'

"Can you believe this crap?" I grab one off the wall and shove it into my friend's faces. "All they want to do is scare the poor souls who haven't found their soulmates yet. It's a disgrace to humankind that we need to conform to a social norm that requires us to fall in love and get married. I'm so sick of this shit."

Sadie takes the flyer from my hand and throws it into the garbage. "Don't stress about Kayleigh, we will find you someone before the deadline comes up. Operation Spencer is still in play."

I'm walking backwards so I can talk to my friends as I navigate through the hallways. "Don't even bother trying. I'd rather go to the Bunker. I don't want to be in a world where everyone is forced into something they don't want to be in." I can feel my eyes swell up because I know part of me wishes I can stay with my friends forever, but the other part tells me not to bother trying because no one has ever lovingly looked at me. *Sometimes it's easier to reject other people so they can't reject you.* "Besides, Spencer already has a soulmate." I point out the bitch as we walk by their lockers. "See he's basically married to the devil already."

"She's practically using him as an accessory at this point." Kate is referring to the idea that she has him wrapped around her arm like her Chanel handbag.

"How is anyone even friends with her? She just looks mean."

"It's called daddy's money babe. No one wants to be on the wrong side of Midrock Falls' princess."

"Very nicely said Reed." I wrap my arm around the boys, and we head off to class.

…

The school day could not have been any longer, the final class of the day had finished and the five of us meet near the parked car. It's a tradition in this friend's group that one Thursday during the year, we take a road trip about an hour away to the only open drive-in movie theatre. Today's showing is the first four scream movies, and we wouldn't miss it for the world. Kate rides with Reed, so I'm stuck third wheeling with Alec and Sadie. It's more Alec third-wheeling Sadie and me because I called 'shotgun' in my bestie's car, and no man will ever get in the way of a shotgun.

My favourite thing about Alec is that he is not afraid to sing a girly song. Regardless of what we play, he will belt out whatever pops up on my playlist. Today's lucky winner is "Girlfriend" by Avril Lavigne. The three of us go line by line until the song is over. Spending time with my friends is probably the one thing I will miss the most after the deadline. No one ever comes out of the Bunker and the idea of never seeing Sadie, Kate, Reed, or Alec ever again terrifies me.

Sadie notices me staring out the window, so she lowers the volume of the radio.

"What's the matter Kayls?" she asks. "What's going on in that beautiful brain of yours."

"I'm just thinking about the deadline."

"Yeah? What about it?" The one thing about Sadie is that she knows when I lie to her, so I don't even bother trying anymore.

"Just the idea that once the deadline comes, I won't see you guys again." I start to feel tears in my eyes, but then Alec grabs onto my shoulder and gives it a slight squeeze.

"Kayleigh, whatever happens, you will always be a part of the friend group, and if anybody can figure out how to fight against the government from within the Bunker, it's you."

"Seriously Kayls, you are the smartest girl we know, I won't lose hope and Alec won't either. So, if we all try, there's no way the government can keep us apart."

I love these guys. "I love you guys."

"We aren't lying little Kay," I give Alec his rightful death glare and we all give each other a small laugh. I want to believe them, I do, but sometimes I wonder if what they are saying is even possible. Is there even a possible way out of the bunker? And why hasn't anyone figured it out yet?

...

Pulling into the drive-in gives me a sense of happiness. I've been smelling the stale popcorn for miles. When we got there Kate and Reed have already secured our usual spot and are lugging the snacks and drinks from the concession stands.

"All right, all right, who's ready for a 'Scream' marathon!"

"I personally can't wait to see Billy Loomis; he is such a babe."

"Kate you are so right. Him being Ghostface just makes him ten times hotter."

"Sadie, I love you, but stop spoiling every movie we see!"

"Oops," she giggles while planting a big kiss on Alec's face. "I forgot you're not very educated in the film world." Alec chases Sadie around the car and picks her up and twirls her around.

"You guys are disgusting. I'm heading to the bathroom; I'll be right back." Sadie looks at me shocked that I just said that, but only real scream fans understand why.

When I get back to the car the movie has already started. I haven't missed much, and I've already seen this several times with Sadie, so I just came to enjoy the company.

Just as I start to get comfortable, I get a notification on my phone. It can't be any of my friends, they are right next to me, definitely not my parents, so that only leaves one more person. I race to grab my phone.

'1 notification: messages: Jackass'

"Yes!" I scream a little louder than I hoped. I get shushed from four different directions. "Sorry," I whisper back.

Jackass: *You leaving me high and dry tonight, Satan?*

Me: *What r u talking about?*

Jackass: *The clinic? it's Thursday.*

Me: *You poor thing*

Me: *You really can't do anything without me.*

Me: *I took an extra shift last week cuz I had plans tnt.*

Jackass: *Damn I was really hoping to make fun of u tnt.*

Jackass: *Guess it'll have to wait.*

Me: U can't roast me over the phone??

Jackass: Better in person. I like seeing that face u make when u get annoyed.

Me: And what face would that be?

Spencer then proceeds to send me a selfie of himself with a cute little annoyed face, and I am blushing.

Me: *I do not look like that*

Jackass: *Yea u do ahahaha*

I send him a picture of me flipping him off, he just likes the message. So, I assume the conversation is over until I get another notification.

Jackass: *Have fun tnt Satan!! Don't miss me too much.*

If I wasn't fully blushing before, my face is officially red, and even though I would hate to admit it, every time I get a text from Spencer, or see him, I get all nervous. He makes me feel butterflies in my stomach. He is seriously starting to grow on me.

Chapter 15
SPENCER

"All better Mills," I finish wrapping up the paw of my favourite little girl. Millie is a miniature Bernese Mountain dog, and she is the cutest little puppy I have ever seen.

I give her head a few pats before I lift her off the table and bring her out front, to her owner. "All set, Mr. Cook. Millie should be up and running in no time." Millie nuzzles her head against my leg, and I give her one more pat.

"Thank you, Spencer, tell your aunt I said hi." I nod in agreement and follow them towards the door. Mr. Cook and

Millie were the last appointments of the day so I locked the front door and turned the close sign over so Kayleigh and I could start cleaning up.

My aunt left a little while ago, because of some emergency back home, we've been volunteering here for a few months now, so she felt comfortable enough leaving the store in our hands. She made sure; all the important appointments were taken care of before heading out. All I had to do was re-dress Millie's paw, from an accident a few weeks back. The poor pup seemed terrified at first, but she got used to me very quickly. I guess my charm doesn't just stop with humans, any female species will love me. Speaking of which, I find myself lurking as Kayleigh struggles to put something away on the top self.

I lean myself against the door frame waiting to see how long I can stand here without her noticing. "You know, Jackass, if you want to stare at me all night, you could at least help put things away." How she knows I'm even standing there, is crazy, because she doesn't even turn around until my chest is practically rubbing against her back. Now, she is looking up at me with her arms pinned to her chest between us. "Still doesn't look like helping." I hear a hitch in her voice, she is breathing a little heavier than before. It brings me much joy making her squirm like this. I reached for what she was trying to put away and placed it on the top shelf. The moment I let go of the bag, I leave my hand up against the shelf next to Kayleigh's face for as long as she lets me.

I'm not sure what this thing between the two of us is, but all I know is I feel comfortable doing it. Nothing in my life has felt more right. My mind runs wild as I stare down into her deep blue eyes. Undressing her layer by layer in my head, thinking of all the things we shouldn't do in this room.

She grunts, and I'm snapped back to reality, I lower my arm and back away from her. "Uh, thanks for the help," she seems genuine, it's a new side of her.

"Of course."

After a moment, I think back to the fact that I still have a girlfriend, and pursuing whatever this is, would be wrong, especially since things are so complicated with Josie right now.

Seriously Spencer now is when you choose to use your moral compass? I try my hardest to stay clear of Kayleigh for the rest of the night while we finish cleaning up, but just when I think I'm in the clear, I hear a loud crash coming from the backroom.

I've never moved quicker in my life, "Holy shit Satan, what'd you do?" I step into the back room, to find Kayleigh on the floor with the dog treat jar shattered around her. "If you wanted something to eat that badly you should've just asked, those are for the dogs." I can't help but laugh a little.

"Are you just going to stand there and make fun of me?" she mutters under her breath. I lend out my hand to help her up, and as soon as our hands touch a mischievous grin appears across her face and she pulls me down next to her. It's her turn to break out into laughter, as we are both sitting on the floor surrounded by crushed-up doggy treats.

"Seriously not cool, even for you." This look of innocence washes over Kayleigh, it would be so easy for me to wrap her in my arms and kiss her.

To have those lips wrapped over mine, we could finally release all the built-up tension between us. But as easy and as amazing as that seems, something in me decides to start getting up. With a look of defeat forming on her face, she reaches out for my arm before I can get away.

"Kiss me."

There's hunger in her eyes, and she can sense the same hunger in me. She leans in close to me, and all my senses defy me. The sweet smell of roses, mixed with the feeling of my fingers interlacing hers, I am ready for whatever this girl throws at me.

"Kiss me."

I lean further back onto the floor and invite her to straddle my lap. Without missing a beat, she drops herself into my lap and moves her hands up the front of my chest. My heart is beating rapidly, and my breath is speeding up as well. She is looking from eye to eye, trying to read me, trying to figure out what the next move should be. Everything she does next is almost picture-perfect. She lets her hair come loose from the messy bun she's been wearing all day and pushes all the hair to one side to show me her neck. I can see her pulse quicken as she leans toward my lips. Her gorgeous blue eyes are looking at me, and she swipes her tongue across her bottom lip. All the blood in my body rushes to where she is slowly grinding; I am now fully hard under these purple scrubs. She reaches her soft delicate hands to the sides of my face, "Kiss me" she begs those two words again. Kissing her is the only thing going through my head right now. Everything in me is telling me I should.

"Kay-." I try talking but she doesn't let the words come out. She lowers her face to mine and we both dive right into the kiss. Her tongue pierces through the opening, my lips give her, and we are both hungry for it. My hands swoop into her hair as her hands travel up my spine. Everything at this moment feels right, but something stops me. *What are you doing?* I reluctantly push myself away from Kayleigh, allowing her to sit on the floor and stand up.

"I'm sorry, but I can't."

She seems so small sitting on the floor, looking up at me with those eyes. I don't know why I stopped, I have been thinking about this moment for so long and I had it, but now it's ruined. *Nice work Jackass.* Even the voice inside my head is telling me how dumb I am.

She stands up in front of me and brushes her scrubs flat. Without saying anything else she walks off past me and grabs her things. *Great job.* She quickly comes back dressed in her normal clothes. She always wears a worn-out band tee and a pair of jeans that are covered in drawings. I love seeing the new drawings she adds every week, she has such an amazing talent.

"Uh, I cleaned up the mess, so I think we are good to go." I'm trying to start up the conversation again, but Kayleigh doesn't seem to care. It's like her mouth was sewn shut after I turned her down. I can't blame her for it, but I wish I hadn't made things awkward.

"Great. Are you good to lock up? I have to be home soon anyways." Before I can even answer, she heads towards the front door. I try following her, but she is too quick, before the door shuts behind her, I yell, "Good night, Satan." *I'm the biggest jackass on this planet.*

I run my hands through my hair and shake my head as I walk back into the clinic.

Kayleigh

Good night, Satan. That's what he says when I walk out of the clinic, are you kidding me? I just made the biggest fool of myself. What on earth was I thinking? Why would Spencer Brown want to hook up with me when he has Midrock Falls' princess, Josie Carson? I get into my car and blast the radio, trying to drown out all the thoughts running through my head.

I pulled into my driveway in record time, the roads were deserted, and I'm grateful because I cannot wait to get into my bed and forget the last hour of my life.

I feel too defeated to even get ready for bed, so I decide to skip the skincare routine Sadie designed for me and hop right into bed. I instinctively pull out my phone, and open the group chat of me, Sadie, and Kate: "The OG three".

Me: Ice cream tmr after skl? :(

Sades: Omg babes what happened?

Sades: Do u need me to come over now?

Me: No need

Me: I'm just really fucking stupid

Kate: what happened?

Me: I kissed Spencer. But he turned me down

Me: it was so humiliating

Sades: NOOO I'm sorry kayls!!

Kate: girls' night after we kick his ass

Sades: oh totally!!

Me: this is why I love you both

I plug my phone in and turn it over. I can feel myself drifting to sleep when I hear another notification ring. I ignore the first one because I assume it's just the girls typing back, but when it rings two more times, I grab the phone in case it was something important.

Notification: messages: Jackass

I tell myself that I am not going to read his messages tonight, but my finger has already clicked on the notification.

Jackass: hey Satan u get home, ok?

Jackass: no answer?

Jackass: I'm sorry about today

Jackass: please don't ignore me

Jackass: fine I get it. Just let me know you got home the roads were pretty shitty.

Jackass: If you don't answer, I'm going to wake up Alex or Reed.

Jackass: You know how much they need their beauty sleep.

Seriously, he is trying to make jokes right now. I'm not going to give him the satisfaction of answering him with words, instead, I just like the first text and throw my phone to the edge of the bed. I feel a slight flutter in my stomach because him worrying, about whether I made it home okay makes me think he cares, but then I remember the look on his face when he pulled away from our kiss, and my heart breaks a little. I hear another notification sound but this time I choose to ignore it.

Hopefully, I can go to sleep and forget that this day ever happened.

Chapter 16

Kayleigh

School flashed by in a total blur, all day I felt like a zombie in my own body. Moving from class to class without mentally being there. Thank God for my friends, the moment I saw them this morning, they could not have been more caring, they have been my eyes and ears all day, taking down the homework, and making sure we don't run into Spencer or Josie, I couldn't appreciate it more. The second we get back into the car after the day of school, Sadie suggests we all meet up at her place. During the day they told me, they had been thinking about my whole soulmate situation. They are convinced we can come up with a way for me to get out of the Bunker if we investigate it together. Even though I feel useless now, Sadie thinks it would be a good way to forget about what happened, so I agree, and we all head to Sadie's house.

Some time has passed since we started working at Sadie's place and I feel like I am sitting in a situation room. We are all spread out in Sadie's room, and she even brought out her giant whiteboard, so we can map out our plan.

"Okay, let's figure out the basics first," you know Sadie is ready to work when she has her hair up in a bun and glasses on. She starts writing down things that could be useful information.

- Has anyone ever gotten out of the Bunker?
- Is there a way to fully avoid the Bunker?
- Can the deadline be pushed?
- Layout of the Bunker

"Is that all?" Alec finds it hard to hide his sarcasm, but I tend to agree with him on this one, seems to be a pretty complicated list.

"Do you seriously think the government would keep any of this information online?" Reed is the one to ask the question we were all wondering.

"Don't be so negative, and besides we have the best computer hacker this town has to offer." Sadie walks over to Kate and gives her a wink.

"I'll take the compliment, but I've tried looking for things like this when Kayls first started talking about not wanting to find her soulmate. I've searched everywhere couldn't find a thing."

"Well, not with that attitude. We will sit here for as long as it takes until the five of us find a solution."

"Reed and I have a baseball game later tonight so we can only sit here for a few hours." Sadie lets out a huge sigh, "Fine, we will sit here, until, we have to leave."

The next two hours pass and the five of us found nearly nothing. I say nearly because Kate found what she thinks could be the layout of the Bunker, but it could take her weeks to decrypt the file. That was the perfect sign to stop our research for today. I rub my eyes with the back of my hands and stare at the work that is scattered in front of us.

"I know it's though Kayls, but there's still some hope." I lean up against my best friend, "You're right, but I don't want to get my hopes up too much. You never know what's going to happen.

...

Somehow my friends have convinced me to leave the house and go cheer on Alec and Reed. Sadie and Kate said they would stay home with me if I wanted to, but I would rather spend time with all of them, so if that means having to go to another baseball game, where I will probably see people I rather not, then that's what it means.

Both Kate and Sadie are wearing their boyfriend's extra jersey, so to ensure I don't feel too excluded, they dress me head to toe in the school's colours. I'm still not one to care about any of the school spirit stuff, but it made my friends happy, so I did it.

We go to park the car and walk the boys to their locker room, before going to find our seats. When we round the corner, Spencer is already standing by the entrance. I tell myself to walk the other way, but Sadie has her arm wrapped around mine, so I'm stuck walking with her. We turn to the boys and wish them luck before they saunter into the locker room.

Before I can turn around, I hear Spencer's voice call my name. "Hey, Satan." I don't acknowledge. He tries another time. "Satan?" Once again, I chose not to answer. I expect him to call my name one more time, but he doesn't. Instead, I feel his hand tap me on the shoulder. I turn around to face him, and my pulse quickens. *Why does he have such a hold on me?* Kate and Sadie share a quick look before they glare into Spencer's soul, and when I motion that I will meet them at the bleachers, I internally yell at myself for letting them go.

"What do you want Spencer."

"You never texted me back last night?"

"Since when do you care if I text you or not."

"I- I just wanted to make sure you got home safe. And we should probably talk about what happened."

"Me getting home safe is none of your business. And as far as I'm concerned nothing happened. The cookie jar fell, and you helped me clean it up. That's it."

"Oh, I mean, I thought-."

"You thought what? That I was another girl who obsesses over you? Get it through your thick skull, Jackass, I don't like you. It was a spur-of-the-moment thing. Don't worry, it won't happen again." Why I feel the need to explain myself is beyond me. I shouldn't even give this guy the time of day, he never gave it to me.

Spencer doesn't respond, so I walk away from him and I don't look back.

I get to the bleachers to find Sadie and Kate. I plop down next to them and let out a huge sigh. "How'd it go?" asks Kate.

"Could've been worse," I can't help but because this whole situation is one giant joke.

The game won't start for another half hour, so I offer the girls that I would go and grab them snacks. They both recite their orders, but I don't listen. I've known them long enough to know that Kate always gets popcorn with gummy bears, and Sadie gets the Kit Kat bar with a raspberry slush. Two very predictable people when it comes to their snacks.

The line isn't super long but concessions at these types of things can take a while, which is not entirely a bad thing because if I miss the start of the game, I won't be too upset. It's nearly my turn when I hear the most irritating voice come from behind me. I can't bring myself to turn around because if I do then she'll be there.

"OMG, you will not believe what Spencer told me this morning." *Oh shit. She can't possibly be talking about me, right?*

Her little disciples are listening to her intently, waiting for her to drop the big news. "Instead of me telling you, how about we ask our dear friend Kayleigh." *Guess she is talking about me. Great.* "What do you want to know bitch, I- I mean Josie?"

"I want to know why you stuck your tongue down my boyfriend's throat?"

"Funny of you to assume it wasn't him kissing me." At this point, I'm going to do anything I can to make Josie feel like shit. Not my finest move, but she does deserve it.

"Why would he do that, when he is dating me?" She honestly makes it too easy sometimes.

"Oh, I don't know, maybe he found out you're not a real blonde. Or that you're stupid and not faking it. Or maybe he used an app to see what you would look like when you're older and saw that you were even uglier than you are now?" That last one gets a few snickers from her minions standing behind her, but she gives them a quick look to stop.

"Let's make something clear, you will never be with Spencer. You won't even get to graduate, because last time I checked, you don't have a soulmate." My blood is boiling, and this girl can sense it. "So, instead of playing hooky with my Spencer, maybe you should spend more time looking for the poor guy who got paired up with you. Unless you want to make this world a better place and head straight to the Bunker now?" She seemed very proud of herself. Her demeanour changes to seem more intimidating, and she looks over to her minions for confirmation to see if her dig was good.

I grab the snacks I had ordered from the counter and look back towards Josie. "If going to the Bunker is the only way that I never have to see a Carson face again, I should've gone years ago." I push past her, and she loses her balance.

"Fuck you, Kayleigh. Careful what you wish for. Be sure to send cards from wherever you end up!" I stick my middle finger straight into the air and walk back to the bleachers.

...

"Josie is such a bitch." Sadie jumps out of her seat. "Want me to kick her ass." I can't help but laugh because we all know Sadie is not much of a fighter.

"Slow down there Rocky, we don't need you breaking a nail tonight." She shoves me a little and sits back down. "Anyways, tonight is about cheering on the boys."

"What did you do with the real Kayleigh?" Kate is looking me up and down, "because she would never say something like that. There was way too much school spirit in those few words."

I flip them the bird and cheer as loud as I can when I spot Alec and Reed running onto the field. The girls both look at each other in disbelief but join me, in cheering the boys on. We are by far the loudest ones in the. All the parents, students, girlfriends, Alec, and Reed had also noticed us, but the only person whose attention I was hoping to catch, is looking directly at me. Spencer is standing in his position, watching me cheer for other guys. I am just cheering for Alec and Reed, but even so, I want a reaction out of Spencer. From here, I can't tell if he looks angry or if he is just focused, but I'm secretly hoping it's the first choice.

Chapter 17
SPENCER

"Come on Spencer, it was just a joke." Josie has been repeating those few words nonstop since we got into the car. "It's not like she didn't deserve it. You told me she came onto you. Why would you care if I called her out?" I roll my eyes at the sound of her excuses. "Seriously Josie? The poor girl is being sent to the Bunker anyways, what makes you think she wants to deal with your nonsense on top of it."

"The poor girl? What is this, are you too friends or something?" I let out a long sigh.

"I'm not saying that."

"So, who cares what I say to her? It's not like anybody likes her. Her only friends are those two losers from your baseball team and their girlfriends. How she managed to be friends with them is beyond me."

"Alec and Reed are the nicest people you could know, so don't even start. Just cool it. Please, for me?" She moves her head against the headrest and looks me in the eyes.

"Whatever Spencer. She's not going to be a problem for me much longer, she'll be gone soon enough."

Getting into arguments with Josie has become a constant endeavour, every time the two of us are together, we always end up disagreeing on something. It's everything we do; whether it's which friends we are going to hang with, or that she thinks I'm not spending enough time with her because of baseball. She somehow finds a reason to complain about every little thing in my life. Even when she knows how important those things are.

When I was younger my parents sat me down to explain to me the whole concept of finding your soulmate, they said, that once you meet them, everything in the world will feel right. That, the person you are destined to be with, fills the gap within you.

I've always loved hearing the story of how they met. It was the day after my mom's twelfth birthday, and she was throwing a party for all her friends. The day of the party arrived, and no one showed up. Turned out, that another kid in her class decided to have their party on the same day. My mom was so upset, she couldn't believe that none of her closest friends came to celebrate with her. She was so keen on leaving, but my grandmother convinced her to stay for a little while longer. Just as my mom was getting ready to give up, my dad walked in with a big box wrapped in pink wrapping paper. Her eyes were so puffy because she had been crying for so long but the smile that appeared on her face made waiting a little longer, worth it.

They became best friends after that moment and were inseparable ever since. Turns out he was heading to the other girl's birthday party, but when he walked in and saw my mom, he realized that this was where he was meant to be.

I have always imagined myself feeling the same way when Josie suggested we start seeing each other. I hadn't felt it then but figured that over time that longing feeling would vanish because Josie is supposed to be the one. Looking back on everything we've been through I now question whether I've made a mistake, but every time I bring this concern up with her, she reassures me that we are soulmates. She takes a lot of pride in having seen the soulmate list on her father's computer, but whenever I ask her if I could see it, she always comes up with some excuse as to why I could not see it.

She told me that instead of us finding each other on our own, she decided to take it upon herself to come find me first.

I pull the car into her driveway and watch her jump out. "You coming in?" I shake my head and tell her that I have a shift at the clinic tonight. She doesn't argue and slams the car door shut, I wave to her and pull away from her house before she even reaches the door.

...

The drive to the clinic took longer than I had expected. The amount of construction on the roads was outrageous. By the time I had gotten to the parking lot of the clinic, I was thirty minutes late.

"Thirty minutes late?" I don't know why I expected to get off easily or think she wouldn't make some comment, "Luckily for you, the owner is your blood relative, so she can't fire you." Kayleigh is sitting at the receptionist's desk, keeping herself entertained with a pen.

"It was all part of the plan Satan," she looks up at me, "Get here late so you can do all the hard work. It's only fair since I do all the work for class." She throws my scrubs toward me, which generates a chuckle. "Go get dressed, Jackass."

"You know-." Kayleigh has already left her spot at the desk when I turn around, I am currently talking to Lianne. "What do I know?" Lianne looks up at me, she knows there is tension between me, and Kayleigh and she is all for it. "Never mind Lianne, I thought you were someone else." My cheeks start to feel a little hot when she knowingly nods in my direction.

I don't run into Kayleigh again until later that night. *The clinic is not that big, so how we don't run into each other is beyond me.* I see her grabbing her things and heading straight for the door.

"You going somewhere?" she jumps at my voice; I don't think she noticed me standing there. "Yup. Finished for the day, was going to go home." She rocks between her two feet; it makes her look uncomfortable standing in front of me. "Anyways," her voice cuts through silence in the air, "I guess I will see you next week." Before she walks out the door, my mouth moves quicker than my brain, and I say the first thing that comes to mind. "I hope Josie didn't make you too insecure the other day."

Abort. Abort.

Her entire body halts in the door frame, as all the air is sucked out of the room.

"What did you just say?" *Crap.*

"I just meant to say that Josie shouldn't have said anything to you."

Kayleigh closes the door, and is standing in front of me in a matter of seconds, glaring into my soul.

"I expect this type of behavior from that bitch you call a girlfriend. But from you? That surprised me."

I try speaking but Kayleigh cuts me off with her finger. "Unlike you, I am mature enough to realize that what happened was a mistake. I did not need you running to your little girlfriend and telling her that I came onto you like a desperate puppy." I am too stunned to speak, I can't tell if it's because this side of Kayleigh scares me, or that having her this close is messing with my head. Before I could figure it out, she is already halfway to her car.

Way to go Jackass.

The feeling that I have when I get home from locking up the clinic is guilt. I thought the two of us were good again. But clearly, I struck a nerve, so I do what any respectable person would do, I text her. I expected her to answer me right away, but when she didn't, I couldn't help the feeling of my ego bruising.

Me: *I'm sorry about tonight.*
Me: *I didn't think you'd react like that*

I finally get a response from her, and when it has her twist of sarcasm embedded into it, I know I didn't just ruin whatever friendship we still possibly had.

Satan: *You seem to always be apologizing for something.*

Me: *I know. I keep messing up.*

Satan: *That is an understatement Jackass.*

Me: *I deserve that, at least ur still using my nickname*

:)

Satan: *Writing Jackass is quicker than writing; person I hate most in the world ;)*

Me: *It's times like these where you think ur funny, but ur not.*

Satan: *Trust me, I'm funny.*

We continue talking for the rest of the night until, I assume, she falls asleep because she stops answering. Having a conversation with her is easy. We can talk about everything and nothing at the same time. We agree that since the deadline is coming up soon, we will refrain from talking about it when we see each other. As much as I would love to pick her brain on the whole concept, I couldn't object because she kept reminding me of all the times I have already screwed up. She also used the fact I kept calling her little Kay, to get me to her terms. I still think it's a cute nickname, but she seems to despise it, so I obliged and let it go.

It's been a while since the two of us have talked like this. I hadn't noticed how much I missed it until I caught myself smiling every time her name popped up on my phone. I don't understand what this girl does to me, but clearly, it's something big.

I turn over in my bed and think back to all the moments I've had with her thus far. The last thing I think of before I fall asleep is her hair tangled in my hands while I'm kissing her on the floor of the clinic. *Kayleigh lives in my head all the time.* And I don't think I mind.

Chapter 18

Kayleigh

Sadie was meant to come and pick me up at my house, so the two of us can spend the day together. She's over an hour late and not answering any of my calls or texts. I decided to walk over because it's honestly not too far, and I don't have the car today. I march up the front steps, and instead of knocking I just grab the spare key, her family leaves under the flowerpot. *They are like my second family. I come and go from this house as I please.* Anyway, I walk up the stairs to announce my arrival.

"Sadie Alexis Silverstein you better have a good reason for standing me up!" I get to her bedroom door and hear people moving things around. I cautiously open the door, and I see a semi-naked Alec trying to zip up the fly of his jeans. His face is flushed, but the poor kid doesn't move.

I do that little whistle all guys know how to do when they see something they like. "Looking mighty fine Rose." He runs his hand through his messed-up hair and tries to sneak past me. He almost manages to get away but not before I slap his ass, baseball style.

"You're not going to let him forget that will you?" Sadie asks as she throws her oversized knit sweater over her head. "You know me too well." I hop onto her bed feeling proud of myself for the way I intruded.

"So, this is why you stood me up?" Sadie, drops her head into her palms, "I'm sorry Kayls I completely forgot I was supposed to pick you up." I'm usually one to hold grudges but never against my best friend, she is an exception to the rule. "Don't worry about it Sades, at least now I have a few more things to haze Alec about."

I've said it a million times and I will keep saying it, Sadie is my best friend, and she knows when something is wrong, or when I'm keeping something from her. We share the same brain, so when I get lost in my thoughts for a few seconds, Sadie jumps all over me about it.

"What's on your mind, babe?" I hop off her bed and start pacing the room. I start finding it hard to breathe and my eyes are swelling with tears. "Kayleigh? What's the matter, you can tell me." My chest feels tight, everything around me is getting smaller, and panic starts to rise in me. This feeling of sheer terror has been a recent thing, and I still haven't found a way to control it.

Sadie has always known how to calm me down, so it doesn't surprise me when she bear hugs me from behind and gently brings us to the floor. She is taking big deep breaths with me, and when I finally regain control of myself, I look towards her. I'm not sure how she hears me, because I barely talk over a whisper, "I've always known that I would end up going to the Bunker, but it hasn't hit me until a week ago."

She grabs the hair that has fallen from my loose braid and tucks it behind my year. "I know you're scared."

For years the two of us have been inseparable. I love Sadie with all my heart, and I know she loves me just as much back. If having a best friend counted as a soulmate, I would've bet everything I own that Sadie and I would be together forever. I think I always knew that one day the two of us would be separated, but I was hoping it would be later in life.

When we were young, we dreamt of growing up together and having connecting houses, so our kids could experience life with their best friends. It wasn't until I decided to boycott the whole soulmate decision that I started imagining all the things Sadie would get to do without me. She gets to experience college, get married to Alec, have kids, and everything the two of us wished to do together, she will experience alone.

"Life without you will never be the same." She has tears dripping down her face, "but if any of us have a chance to survive the mystery that is the Bunker it's you Kayls." I wrap my arms around my best friend for what feels like an eternity.

"Ok, can we now stop being all sentimental, we both look like puffer fish." Sadie slaps my arm, and a grin tugs the side of her mouth. "Shut up Kayls."

Hours fly by before either of us starts talking again. You know you're good friends when you can sit in complete silence for hours without being bored. I was busy painting one of Sadie's old pair of jeans when she jumped up to show me a text from Kate.

Kate: *The first part of the decryption worked! I'm waiting for the rest of the map to generate.*

Sadie: *OMG Kate ur the best.*

Kate: *I know! :)*

Sadie: *I'm with Kayls right now and she is beaming!!*

I hear another notification go off, but Sadie is quick to hide her phone. I sense the energy in the room changing and when she doesn't immediately tell me what Kate had just sent her, I pry it out of her.

"Sadie, what did she just text you?" There's hesitation in her voice, "It's nothing Kayls don't worry about it."

"Don't lie to me," my voice is stern, this is not the time to keep things from me. I can see her thinking of what she wants to say to me, and when she finally spills it, I almost fall to the ground.

Fuck.

This can't be happening.

The final part of the decryption is going to take longer than Kate was hoping. The timeline she estimated was the day of the deadline. *I'm screwed.* My face turns white, as the words leave Sadie's mouth.

There isn't anything we can do now but wait and hope. Sadie reassures me that even if the decryption doesn't finish in time, the rest of them will find a way to help me from the outside. I want to believe her, I do, and I know they will do their best, but, if I don't get this map, I better at least enjoy the last few days I have with them.

CHAPTER 19

SPENCER

I feel a burst of excitement when I turn into the parking lot of the vet clinic. I've been fighting the urge to get here early all day. Something inside me keeps wanting to be sitting at the reception desk when Kayleigh arrives. I want to be the first thing she sees when she walks in the door. After the two of us made up, or should I say Kayleigh forgiving me for being a total "jackass" we've been talking almost every day. *Over the phone of course.* I could not risk Josie finding out about me being friends with the "enemy". I must give it to Kayleigh though, until this year I never really knew who she was, unless Josie was talking shit about some girl, she used to be friends with. But Kayleigh is genuinely one of the nicest people I know.

Yeah, she can be extremely sarcastic at times, and sometimes I wonder if she is even being sarcastic or if she truly hates me. I'm going to stick with the sarcastic bit, not only for my ego, but- *no who am I kidding, it's all about the ego.*

I sigh a breath of relief when I don't notice Kayleigh's car in the parking lot, this could mean two things.

- She still hasn't gotten here yet.
- Someone else drove her.

I'm secretly hoping for both, because then I can see her walk in, but if someone drove her then she would have to ask for a lift home. I want to give her a lift home, all I've been thinking about is being near her again. Even though she said she forgave me, and we are friends over text, I still feel a cold shoulder every time I see her at school. Especially in biology class, given that Josie is also in the class, our conversations never veer far from the lab we are doing. If we were to go off-topic, and accidentally laugh a little too loud, I can feel the glares emerging from Josie's desk. Have I mentioned my girlfriend can sometimes be psychotic?

I walk into the building, and to my relief, she is not here yet. I make a mental note to nag her for showing up later than me. I quickly grab my purple scrubs from the back room. I once accidentally grabbed Kayleigh's, they were too small, but I just thought the work I was putting into the gym all year made me a few sizes bigger. It wasn't until Kayleigh walked into the back with a baggy set of scrubs that I realized I grabbed the wrong ones. Ever since then, she has been adding these small designs to them, so it never happens again. I was expecting my aunt to be sterner when it came to uniform, but she thought it brought out her style, so she let it be.

That's another thing I hadn't expected from her. Her artistic abilities are better than anyone I've ever seen. She can draw all these amazing pictures, yet I can barely draw a stick figure. It's a bit unfair.

I notice an unfamiliar car pull into the parking spot right out front and see a whole gang of people hop out of the car. It is not until they are walking through the door, do I notice my baseball buddies walking behind Kayleigh and her best friend, I had asked Alec what her name was because I kept forgetting. *I should know it since Kayleigh talks about her all the fucking time. It's cute.*

"So, this is the famous clinic?" Reed does a spin in the middle of the room to take in the clinic and all its glory.

"What's up Rivers," I call from my spot. These are two guys I wish I had become friends with off the field, but Josie never let that happen. She has always been very particular as to who she lets in her friend group, the moment she realized they were friends with Kayleigh, that was the end of a potential friendship.

"Guess we know who Spence's favourite is," you can visibly see a pout form on Alec's face. "I was getting to you, Rose." I stand up to properly say hi to them. "Where's your better half, Reed?" He shrugged his shoulders, but Sadie informed me that she was working on something extremely urgent. I can tell that she isn't going to elaborate so I leave the conversation at that.

I hadn't noticed until now that Kayleigh had snuck away to change into her scrubs, when she walks back into the main area, I'm quick to nag her. "You're late Satan," I say in a mocking tone, I get the reaction I desire because she rolls her eyes at me before shoving me out of the way. "Did you seriously need the whole squad to come and drop you off?"

"First off, I cannot believe you just used the word squad. Are you twelve?" she's standing in between Sadie and Reed wrapping her arms around their shoulders, "And second, they insisted on dropping me off."

Reed speaks up now, "It's true bud, we've been wanting to see where she spends her Thursdays."

"We've also been spending as much time with her as possible since deadline day is next week." Alec tries saying it nonchalantly, but the mood quickly changes when the comment fills the room. I always thought Kayleigh was fine with the whole, not having a soulmate thing, but we don't talk about it anymore.

"Well on that note, we should leave them to it." Sadie is practically pushing the boys out of the clinic; they are bigger than she is, but she doesn't struggle at all. It's clear that they are letting her do it, but I still find it amusing.

Before the door closes, Sadie asks Kayleigh if she needs them to pick her up after she is done. Without thinking or asking, I told her that I would give her a lift home. This puts a sheepish grin on her best friend's face before she skips her way to the car.

"What makes you think I want a lift home with you?"

"Do you not want one? Cause you could walk."

"Well since you sent away my other option, I guess I will put up with you for one more car ride. But only if I get aux."

"And I thought you would come with me because of how close we are." My sarcasm is seeping through the walls, but it gets her laughing, which always makes me feel good.

Working at the clinic has helped me figure out that this is something I would consider as a career path. Figuring out what is bothering the animal and then treating it is a full-circle moment that I want to experience daily. I'm extremely grateful that I was able to volunteer here this year. I grew up coming here after school some days when my aunt was not too busy so she could show me the ropes of things, and I couldn't wait until I was finally able to apply for a volunteering position through the school. I know I chose this opportunity because I can see myself doing this in the future, but I cannot wrap my head around the idea that Kayleigh knows she doesn't have a future to look forward to. *Damn that's harsh.* So why would she want to volunteer here?

That question lingers in my head for the entire shift. We both agreed to stay late for our final shift together, so when my aunt finished up for the day, she came to find us. She is not the type of person to become sentimental with goodbyes or anything, but I can tell that she appreciates the work that the two of us put in. I swear I even see some tears forming when she hugs Kayleigh goodbye. I can't help but think of the discussions the two of them had when I wasn't here because I would occasionally see the two of them deep in conversation. Kayleigh got close with Lianne as well, I'm happy she opened up to them, they are both great listeners and give killer advice.

It's finally just the two of us. We stay silent during the shift because we both want to show Patty how "professional" we are. Even though we both knew that she couldn't get rid of us since we were the only two to sign up.

"Yo Satan!" I call from the back room. When I hear her tiny footsteps approach, I peek out the door.

"You hollered my lord?" She mockingly bows her head as a sign of respect.

"Yes, I did."

She looks me up and down waiting for an explanation as to why I just yelled for her. To be honest, I don't even know why I called her, but I got to think of something quick because her patience is running thin.

"I thought maybe we could talk?"

"Talk? As in communicate?"

"Yes?" I question where she is going with that.

"What a great idea, Jackass, no one could've come up with that concept all by themselves." This girl finds pleasure in making me feel like a fool, there's this twinkle in her eye whenever she says something like that.

"Well, you didn't have to be so mean about it." She giggles as she leans against the door frame with her arms crossed.

We sit in silence for a few seconds before she decides to break it. "So, what did you want to talk about?"

"Oh, honestly anything."

"Well, that's specific." I think I'm losing her; I need to come up with something quickly.

"Why don't we talk about the deadline?" All the colour in her face fades away. I've never seen her like this before. Tears start rolling down her face, her breath becomes shaky, and I'm not sure how to make it stop. *Great job.*

I do not know how to console her, I feel horrible, I don't even know where this came from, she always seemed so strong when we used to talk about the deadline and all the soulmate stuff. I always admired her for not giving a flying fuck about it. But clearly, something happened, because before I can even fathom a response to her reaction, she is already walking out of the room heading for the front door.

I decide to follow her, my strides are bigger, so it doesn't take me long to catch up to her. When we step outside, we are immediately hit with rain. We aren't even outside for long, but we are both drenched. I give her the space she needs until she decides to turn around to face me. I can no longer tell what the tears are and what the rain is. I know she is crying because her eyes are red and puffy. I debate reaching out for her to hug her or if it is better to back off. I ultimately decided to just stand in front of her and let her open herself up to me. It's a good thing I decided to refrain from that because she started talking.

"Why did you have to bring up the deadline?" Her voice is frail, I feel awful that this is my fault. I made her feel like this, and it caused a sudden pain in my chest.

"I'm sorry. I didn't think you would react this way. You always talked about how you never agreed with the soulmate stuff, so I figured you had this badass plan on how you would walk into deadline day."

"Did it ever occur to you that, maybe just maybe I don't want to disappear forever? I still want to be able to see my friends and family. The entire concept of having a soulmate is bullshit. Everyone knows it but no one will ever say anything. A soulmate doesn't need to be someone you fall in love with. A soulmate should be someone you care about, someone you can count on no matter what," her voice cracks after every sentence, but the last thing she says sticks with me, "someone willing to sacrifice themselves, so you can continue."

I repeat those words in my head. I think about Josie, and if she would do all this if I needed her? Would I do all this if she needed me? I don't have an answer, I truly cannot stand here and confidently say that either one of us would stand in front of a bullet for the other person.

When I look back towards Kayleigh, I can't help but notice her shivering. I wrap my arms around her and guide her back into the warmth of the clinic. I give her some space so she can go change out of her wet clothes. When she comes back, she looks tired, but at the same time relieved.

Maybe she's been holding all that in for quite some time. If she was, I am happy she felt comfortable enough to open up with me.

During the time that Kayleigh was changing, I finished up with closing the clinic. I figured she would have wanted to leave after she changed so I made sure everything was done. The mood of the night has shifted, but I don't want to end the night this way. We both get into my car, and I pass the aux chord to Kayleigh. I know it's not saying much but I could tell she appreciates the gesture. I put the car into drive and started pulling out of the parking lot. I make a swift decision to turn right instead of left. She looks up with concern in her eyes.

"Trust me?" she doesn't say a word, she just nods her head, and that's all the response I need to continue driving.

We've been driving for about thirty minutes, but it feels longer, the only noise around us is the music coming from the radio. By the time we got to the destination the rain has fully subsided, and the sky was clear. She looks confused as to why we are here. I put the car into park and hop out. She hesitantly follows my lead.

"What are we doing up here?"

I walk over to the edge of the cliff and sit on the ground. "I used to come here a lot when I was younger. The view has always calmed me down."

She walks over towards me and sits down right beside me. "I didn't even know Hidden Ville had views like this."

"There's a lot about Midrock Falls that you've probably never seen. But that's not the only reason I brought you up here." I can hear her breath hitch, "You see that building out in the distance?"

She follows my finger to the industrial-like building meters away. "That's the Bunker."

She seems surprised that the thing she is so afraid of, is so visible from city limits. The building is not tall, but it goes on for a while, the most eerie part about it all, is that there is nothing but trees and empty land surrounding it. We can see the armed fences that restrict people from not only coming in but also leaving. From what you can see, there is only one way in and one way out, but that's not the case.

Kayleigh seems to notice the same thing, "There's only one way in and out." She sounds defeated, "Is there even a chance of someone escaping that place?" I can't tell if she is asking me the question, or if it was simply rhetorical.

"From what I know, there has only been one person to ever escape the Bunker." She looks at me with hopeful eyes, but they quickly fade when I tell her that no one ever heard from him again. "I'm not sure if this helps or not but his name was Mason Clark." I can see the wheels turning in her head, trying to come up with a plan.

"You know you don't have to figure this out alone, right?"

"Of course not, Sadie, Alec, Reed and Kate have been working nonstop trying to figure out a way for me to survive this."

"I can help them if you want. I can tell them about Mason Clark."

"As much as I appreciate it, Spencer, I can't ask you to do that, especially if we take into consideration your girlfriend."

"No, no, I'm offering to help, and if Josie makes a big deal about it, then I will deal with the consequences."

"Thank you."

"Of course." We sit quietly next to each other as it slowly gets later during the night, the cool air is becoming more frigid, and I can see Kayleigh start to shiver. "We can leave if you want to."

"No, it's alright. It is peaceful up here; I can see why you like it." I have never taken anyone up here before, but I figured it would do her some good.

"Why doesn't anyone ever leave this place?" Her question throws me off guard.

"Sorry?"

"There must be other towns out passed city limits, so why hasn't anyone ever left?"

"I've never really thought about it."

"What's stopping me from leaving in the middle of the night and never looking back?"

"For all we know nothing is stopping you, but for me the fear of the unknown would make me want to stay."

"Shouldn't that make me excited though? Having the chance to start over?"

"I guess that could be cool. But no one ever leaves Midrock Falls, the government has made it seem like nothing else is out there. And I guess no one ever wanted to go out and explore it for themselves."

"If you could start over, what would you do?"

"I wouldn't be afraid to open up to people. Make a solid group of friends, like what you, Sadie, Kate, Alec, and Reed have. You guys are a tight group, and to be honest, I'm jealous of it."

"Why?"

"Why am I jealous?" She nods. "I don't have people to talk to, or someone I could trust with how I'm feeling. All my 'close friends' only care about their popularity status, and honestly I could not care less about all that superficial stuff."

"I never would've guessed that you were jealous of us. You hide it well."

"Well, I have had plenty of time to practice."

"But you shouldn't have to pretend to like all the popular stuff, if people don't like you for you, then they aren't worth your time, or energy."

"Thanks Satan."

"I'm serious, don't let people make you feel that way."

"Okay, I won't." She visibly looks upset, and that's the last thing I want her to be. I slide myself closer to her and wrap my arm around her shoulder. She leans into the hug and places her head on my shoulder.

"What if we got back into the car and just drove as far as we could out of the city?"

Kayleigh lifts her head off my shoulder, "We can't."

"Why not?"

"It's like you said, people don't leave this place, so why start now. I couldn't leave my friends, my parents, and my sister without saying goodbye. And even if I do, who knows what will happen to them if the government finds out. I would not want them getting in trouble because of me. I wouldn't be able to live with myself if something were to happen to the people I love."

"I'm sure they would understand."

"You're probably right, but they shouldn't have to deal with the repercussions over something I did. I decided a long time ago, I had zero interest in finding a soulmate, so I kind of dug myself my own grave with this one."

"Do you regret not looking for your soulmate?"

"Obviously, I regret it now, but in the moment, I thought it was the best thing for me. Looking back, I was wrong, and I feel bad for whoever was my soulmate, because they will also be sent to the Bunker, and they never got the choice."

Kayleigh places her head back onto my shoulder and we sit staring into the distance for a little while longer. Eventually the night gets colder, so the two of us head back to the car. Before we reach the car door, she looks over at me, with her beautiful blue eyes glaring into mine, and she whispers, "Thank you for bringing me here."

"Of course." She is still looking at me, and I can't bring myself to look away. She licks her bottom lip and leans in towards me. I grab the sides of her face to stop her from getting too close. I tell myself to push her away, but I can't. I stare into each of her eyes, thinking that this is what I've been waiting for. I forget everything else at that moment. The only thing in my mind is the way her lips felt on mine the first time we kissed; it was electric. I bring her face closer to mine and the second our lips touch, everything feels right in the world. She runs her hands through my hair, and it feels so good.

I am very pleased when we stumbled back to the car, I had moved my seat all the way back before I had gotten out of the car. She leans me back against the seat and lowers herself onto my lap. The immediate feeling of her on top of me triggers my dick in the most amazing way possible. She quickly resumes kissing me, with even more desire than before. Her tongue grazes the part between my lips, and I grant her access. Our tongues meet in an animal-like kiss that has been built up for months. She is grinding against my crotch, and I can't help but let out a moan. I can feel her smile from against my lips. I pull back just enough to look at her sitting on my lap. I reach for the bottom of her shirt, and she helps me lift it off her. To my delight, she is not wearing a bra.

To make things even, I pull my shirt over my head with my free hand. I travel the length of her neck all the way to her shoulder.

"You have no idea how long I've been wanting to do this." She grabs my hand and places it on one of her perky breasts, I look at her to ensure that this is what she wants. When she says to continue, I grab her nipple in my mouth and start sucking on the bud. She grabs my hair and moans with delight.

Every day that I thought about this girl becomes entirely worth the wait because she truly is amazing. It's only until I drop her off at home, that I realize that this may have been the only time the two of us could be together like this. In a week's time, we will both be faced with the deadline. She will be declaring no soulmate, and I will be taking the test to prove that my soulmate is not the amazing girl sitting next to me but my girlfriend, Josie. As much as I would love to risk everything to pick Kayleigh, I can't. Even though Josie may not deserve anything, I have still been with her for years. We have talked about this day for far too long.

It's at this moment I decide that I choose Josie, the girl I once had feelings for, even though it means I may never see Kayleigh again.

Chapter 20

Kayleigh

It's May fourth.

My alarm goes off, but I was already awake. The nerves that I felt last night before going to bed, have subsided. I rummage through my room for the outfit I knew I was going to want to wear. My favourite worn-out Rolling Stones band tee, paired with the jeans I have been painting all through the year. Each design represents another person in my life who has made any sort of difference.

A monarch butterfly for Sadie.

A baseball bat and glove for Alec and Reed.

A bouquet of flowers for Kate.

A locket for my sister, Stella.

A music note for my parents.

And a paw print, that I added a few days ago, for Spencer.

I'm just about ready to walk downstairs when I realize this could be the last time I see my room. I walk out the door, and face the room I've grown up in. Taking it all in for one last time, I close my eyes and close the door. My feet feel stuck to the ground. Something in me refuses to walk away. The sound of the doorbell awakens me from my train of thought. Sadie, Kate, Alec, and Reed texted me last night that they wanted to spend the morning with me before it was too late. Knowing that my best friends and my family are waiting downstairs for me, I finally grow the courage to leave the comfort of my door. When I turn around, I feel like a completely different person. I plaster a smile onto my face and head downstairs.

My thought process is if I look okay, everyone will need to try and put on a brave face. So that's what I did. I take one step at a time and pretend that nothing was wrong.

My parents are insane. I walk into the kitchen to see every single one of my favourite meals lining the counters. There are stacks of chocolate chip pancakes and a mountain of crispy bacon. They made eggs four ways and mixed all the fruit I love into one giant fruit salad. I was always a big breakfast girl; I could eat it all day and every day.

"My god Mom, did you buy out every grocery store in town?" I walk over to her and plant a kiss on the side of her head.

"I wanted you to have a variety of choices," she says with a half-hearted smile. I know this is tough for her, but I wish she wouldn't show it on her face as much.

My dad on the other hand is better at dealing with his emotions. He is finishing the cooking when he chirps from behind the stove. "Your mother did go to several stores just to find the proper bacon."

I look at her as if to tell her she is nuts, but I appreciate what she did for me today.

My friends are all lined up behind the table, not knowing what to do. They all seem to think that if they say the wrong thing, I'll snap. I decided to clear the air, so this last breakfast together could be somewhat normal.

"All right, before this gets too awkward, today is deadline day. I am very aware of the circumstances. I will be declaring no soulmate. I will be taken to the Bunker, and I am very, very nervous about it," I haven't taken a breath of air since I started this little monologue, "but right now we are going to pretend that none of that is happening." I take a deep breath before I ask, "Is that clear?"

Everyone looks at each other and they collectively nod their heads. "Not a problem little Kay." I look at Alec with murder in my eyes, "I guess I don't get a free pass on that do I?" He looks quite scared asking that question but raises his hands in front of his chest when I nod in agreement, not letting him get away with it. If I'm being honest, I truly don't mind it. I got used to it a while ago but watching him squirm every time he says it brings me pleasure. He is way too easy to scare. I love it. However, I promised myself never to tell him. It would boost his ego far too much, and we can't have that.

The next few hours are amazing. We all sit and eat, talking about anything and everything.

"You can't be serious?"

"I'm dead serious Kayls, Reed told me the other day that he wants to name our kids after you." I look over to Reed who is stuffing his face with bacon.

"Damn, Rivers, I didn't take you to be a sentimental guy."

He lifts his arms in protest. "It's okay Reed, you have my blessing to name your kids after me." I can't even get through it without breaking out into laughter. These guys kill me.

"Come on Kate, you said you weren't gonna say anything." She almost falls out of her chair she is laughing so hard.

I get up from my chair and run around to Reed. I hug him from behind and mess with his hair.

"Why are you smiling like that?"

"I just love you guys." They all look back at me with smiles lined across their face. Before I can say another word, they are all up from their seats, coming toward me for a giant bear hug. I can barely breathe, but I let myself sink into the hug. A giant flash nearly blinds us all, and I look over towards my mom and dad, who are holding a vintage Polaroid camera.

"Don't mind us," she chirps, "I just wanted to capture this moment."

We all look at each other with the same idea in our heads, within seconds we gather my parents and share one more hug.

I look around the room and notice that someone is missing. It's my sister. She never came downstairs for breakfast, so I excuse myself for a moment and run up the stairs.

I knock on her door, but no one answers.

"I'm coming in." I slowly push the door open to see my sister holding onto a teddy bear I had given her many years ago.

"Hey Stell," she is trying to wipe the tears from her face, "What's the matter?" She doesn't want to look at me, but I climb into the bed next to her.

"I know you're sad right now, but you are going to have to take care of my room when I'm gone. I can't have Mom and Dad snooping around, can I?" A tiny smile crosses her face. "There's that pretty smile I love."

"It's not fair that you have to leave."

"I know," she reaches out for my hand, and I give it a squeeze, "but I promise everything will be all right."

"How can you promise that if you aren't gonna be here anymore."

"Even though I may not be here, you still have so many people that love you. All my friends have already said you can call them whenever you feel like it. Anything that you need to talk about, whether it's an issue with a friend or a boy, or if you just need an older sibling they will be there in an instant."

"Even Reed?" I let out a laugh. "Yes, even Reed." It must run in the family because even my sister has a massive crush on Reed. Both he and Kate know about it, and they find it really cute.

I reach around my neck and take off the locket I have been wearing and wrap it around her neck.

"Your locket?"

"I need you to keep it safe for me all right? Every time you look at it, it'll be like me being here with you." We share a long hug and stay in her bed for a little while longer until we both decide to walk downstairs hand in hand.

I spoke to my mom and dad a few days ago, about saying goodbye to them at home instead of having them drive me. They were hesitant but understood that I wanted to drive in with my friends.

"I love you so much sweetie," my mom is tucking my hair behind my ears, "whatever happens, we are always thinking of you." Her eyes are glossy, but she is trying her best not to cry. I give her one last hug, "Thank you so much for everything you have done. I love you."

I know my dad doesn't do well with all the sentimental stuff. He never has. He tends to hide all emotion from the people he loves. Something about not wanting to show weakness? Anyways, I walk over to him and say my goodbyes, before heading out of the front door. My friends gave me some space to say goodbye. I quickly wipe my tears from my face before heading to the car.

I peer back toward the door before Sadie starts pulling away. I see my parents finally losing all restraints they have been keeping all morning and my sister holding on to the necklace I just gave her. They are comforting each other, as they watch the car slowly drive away.

The location where we need to be is about an hour's drive from my house, so that's plenty of time to listen to all my favorite songs and forget about what's about to happen.

Sadie is driving, while the other three are squishing in the backseat of the car. Usually, when we drive all together, the guys sit in the front and Alec drives the car. The girls are smaller so it's more comfortable in the back, but they all agreed that I should take the front. I didn't give them another chance to change their minds.

They have already programmed all my favorite songs. One Direction, followed by Taylor Swift, followed by The Rolling Stones, followed by The Beatles. It's like they know me or something. We get through about thirty minutes of music before I decided to shut the radio off.

"What was that for? I was seriously into that."

"We know Alec," Kate is shoving him to the side, "you've been squishing me this entire time."

"Even though I sometimes love my music, more than I love you guys," the guys raise their arms in protest, "I feel like we should just talk for the rest of the trip.

"I think that's a great idea." Kate reaches forwards and places her hand on my shoulder to give it a gentle squeeze.

"Great! Now someone please start talking."

They proceed to tell me all about their baseball season, and how they really have a chance at winning in the playoffs. I surprise myself and get excited for them. I'm obviously going to miss it but I'm sure my boys will do great. Kate tells me how she has been working on her computer skills, and how she thinks they can hatch a plan to help me out of the Bunker. I try not to show my disappointment because I do not want to have high hopes, so I just listen to her ramble on about all thing's technology. It's not until we pull into the parking lot that I realize Sadie has barely spoken to me this entire morning.

The building is a lot bigger when you are standing right in front of it. I've only ever seen the Bunker once before now. My mind flashes back to a few nights ago with Spencer, and how he brought me here when he saw I was scared. I thanked him for that night several times over text, but I only got a quick "no worries" text back. I took it as a sign. I thought he felt something with the kiss, but who am I kidding, he already has a soulmate, and I spent all my time telling him that I don't believe in the system our government tried to put in place. I decided at that moment to take the memories we did have and move forward.

We are all standing outside the car, no one wanting to be the first to say goodbye. I take it upon myself to start. I make my way through each person telling them how much I love every one of them. When I get to Sadie, she can barely look at me. She walks off towards the building and I ran up behind her.

"You haven't said a word to me all morning Sades. What is going on?" I'm standing right in front of her now. She looks distraught.

"I thought that once I actually start saying goodbye then this would be real."

I wrap my arms around my best friends. "This is as real as it'll ever be." We both have tears running down our faces, neither one of us knows how to handle this situation.

We have been best friends from the day we were born, neither one of us expected we'd have to say goodbye to each other so soon. Our dreams of growing old together, and watching our kids become friends are taken away by this day.

I take a step back from Sadie, and I just look at her. This is the last time we may ever be near each other, and my whole body just hurts. I can't believe I am saying goodbye.

"Don't even say it, Kayleigh." She has managed to control her breathing. I know exactly what she means. I give her one more hug before whispering in her ear so only she can hear, "Until next time."

We never liked using the word goodbye, it felt too final, so instead we say, "Until next time". Normally the circumstances work, but if we both have a little faith, then maybe, just maybe we could see each other again.

Before I walk off towards the doors that separate the building and the outside world, Kate runs up to me. She gives me a tight squeeze before reaching into her back pocket and pulling out a small folded- up piece of paper. I give her a questioning look. She leans in close so no one else hears her.

"This is all the information I was able to get off the decrypted site. It looks like some sort of map, but it's hard to tell. I was hoping you'd be able to figure it out once you get inside."

I take the paper from her hand, and I place it in my bra strap. I figure that if they were to search me that's one place they wouldn't think to check.

"We won't give up on finding a way for us to help you from here."

"I trust you guys." I give her a last hug before walking away from my friends.

I tell myself not to turn around. If I do, I don't think I'll be able to stop whatever emotion comes flooding to the surface. My heart is breaking with every step I take toward the doors that separate my future and my past. Right before I walk through them, I reluctantly turn back to see the people who mean the absolute world to me, standing just several feet away with tears flooding down their faces. Nothing I can do to console them, but at least they have each other. As I turn back around, it's at that moment that I see him for the last time. A lean but muscular silhouette of the man I constantly have on my mind every night before I fall asleep and every day when I wake up. All the things I wish I did or wish I had said fade from my mind as the large steel doors close, separating me from the only place I ever called home.

SPENCER

I regret not going to see her before she walked through the doors. She saw me standing here, and all I could do is give her a comforting smile as she walked away forever. I wanted to say something, I really did, but it wasn't the right time or place. It was her moment with her best friends, it would have been wrong of me to disturb their goodbyes.

"There you are!" I say as I notice Josie walking towards me, "We were supposed to go in a few minutes ago."

"It's fine, Spence. You need to relax a bit." She notices my eyes looking past her head. "What a bunch of crybabies. They should really do that somewhere more private, no one wants to see that."

"They just said goodbye to Kayleigh, be a little respectful." My tone is sharp, and she is taken aback by it.

"If you care so much then go stand over there with them," my eyes roll to the back of my head. Sometimes I do not understand how we are compatible. She is so ignorant to others while I have sympathy, but somehow, she's my fated love, so dealing with her is non-negotiable.

We walk towards the doors that Kayleigh had just gone through. I feel my heart beating a bit faster the closer we get to the doors. Josie on the other hand, is looking as cool as a cucumber. When I reach for her hand, she pulls it away. Once through the doors, we are ushered in separate directions. One side for the boys and one side for the girls. I am put in a long queue, that takes around 15 minutes to get to the front. I am faced with an old lady sitting at a desk. She smells of whiskey and cigars, with a short red bob framing her face. She looks quite scary, but her voice is very soothing.

"What are you declaring hon?"

"Um-." The words are in my head but aren't coming out of my mouth.

"You declaring soulmate or no soulmate? It's an easy question." She has a point; I don't know why I'm so nervous."

"Sorry about that, I'm a bit nervous," I let out a small chuckle, "I'm declaring soulmate."

She places a blue sticker on a piece of paper and hands it to me. I'm now being directed toward a waiting area where people are being called into what looks like an interrogation room. The waiting room is painted a dull grey colour, with very little sunlight and no paintings on the wall. It's almost like a prison. Boys are being called in one by one like clockwork. Soon enough I hear my name being called over the P.A. system. I take that as my cue to get up from my seat and head towards the door that had just flung open. I take a seat in the middle of the room and the lights shoot on.

"Please state your name, your declaration, and who you believe to be your soulmate."

"Spencer Brown, I am declaring a soulmate," everything in me wants to say Kayleigh's name. Every time I'm with her I feel something I never felt with Josie. She made me feel like me, not like a puppet for her own amusement. It's taking me a while to answer. I can't tell if it's a real person or a computer asking the question. When they ask the question again, I make my decision.

"Please state your name, your declaration, and who you believe to be your soulmate."

"Spencer Brown, I am declaring a soulmate, her name is Josie Carson." That's my answer. Josie Carson is the girl I picked.

Several minutes go by before I hear the voice again.

"Spencer Brown, we are afraid you have declared the wrong soulmate, please follow Officer Reynold to the holding facility before entering into the Bunker."

Did I hear them correctly?

Did they just say I declared the wrong person?

This cannot be right Josie told me she knew we were soulmates. How could this be possible? My brain is moving twenty miles a minute.

When I don't stand up, the officer who has just entered the room lifts me to my feet and walks me towards the door. My eyes take a while to adjust but I am outside again. I am surrounded by a gate, but I can see the front of the building. My feet are moving but my body still hasn't been able to adjust to the news. Before being placed in confinement, I see Josie standing on the other side of the fence. I want to call out for her, how could she be on that side if I'm here?

It's not until I see who walks up beside her, that all the pieces fall into place.

That little prick.

Josie is standing arm-in-arm with that fucking asshole, Colin. I saw them together so many times but never imagined that they would screw me over like this. What did I ever do to Josie that would make her want to do something so evil?

That's when it hits me.

Josie was telling me at the start of the year that she vowed to make her ex-best friend's life a living hell. That she would fuck with her soulmate selection. She had access to all the soulmates, so she knew who everyone's soulmate was. Her only way to get back at her was to "steal" her soulmate. I almost collapse when I realize what I just figured out...

Kayleigh.

Is.

My.

Soulmate.

All the encounters we had. The feelings I felt for her that I never felt for Josie, everything is starting to make sense. I hate myself for not realizing it sooner. I cannot believe I allowed Josie to convince me that she was the one for me. Everyone around us knew. Mrs. W. had said something about us working well together, her friends kept nagging her about me being her soulmate. For fuck's sake, I even thought we were soulmates. Knowing that someone could purposefully screw someone's life over, makes me question humanity. Then again, our government is sending teens without a soulmate to a place called the Bunker. What is wrong with people?

Once I get into the Bunker, I must find Kayleigh. Explain to her everything that happened. Maybe if the two of us find each other in the Bunker, they would let us leave. Now you're hoping for a miracle. But it is worth a shot.

I think back to when I was watching Kayleigh say bye to her friends. It's not until now do I remember seeing her stuff something into her shirt that Reed's girlfriend, Kate, gave her. She had mentioned something the last day we were together, that they had been looking for a way out of the Bunker. Maybe that's the key.

I need to find Kayleigh.

Fast.

I don't know how much time we have when we get into the Bunker.

Chapter 21

Kayleigh

As soon as I stepped foot into the building, everything around me felt robotic. The people working there looked like they'd been working for years nonstop. They look tired and weak. But they get through each person like clockwork. Once I got through the preliminary line and was directed towards a vacant kiosk, I was asked whether I would be declaring a soulmate or not, my initial answer must not have been quick enough, because the lady sitting behind the desk asked me again.

Everything inside of me screams to say that I have a soulmate, tell them that Spencer is the one, and maybe everything will work out. I can walk out of here with Spencer at my side, and everything will be perfect.

I just couldn't do that to him. Why should I risk him being taken to the Bunker because I couldn't let go of the idea of him? He made his decision, and he picked Josie, not me. I just need to forget about it and face this new reality.

When I finally declared "no soulmate," I was ushered into another line. This line brought me to an isolated hallway filled with rows of rooms. When one of the doors in the hallway swings open, I'm quickly directed towards it. The walls of the room were padded from top to bottom with a cotton-like material. The only exit was the door I was brought through. The room was nearly empty, not even a chair for me to sit on. The only thing that could be found in the room was a neatly folded pile of clothes placed right in the middle. I walk over to the clothes, I hear a muffled voice echo within the small space, it comes from what I assume to be a hidden speaker,

"Change and wait until further instructions."

I lift my thumb in the air. "Thanks." Luckily being here still hasn't taken away my sarcastic ability. It's my only form of defense in awkward situations like these. I strip down in the middle of the room without thinking twice. I've never been one to be ashamed of my body, so I have no trouble changing in front of whatever camera may be in here. Still, I don't waste time and change rather quickly. The shirt is baggy and boring; it's a beige colour with my name stitched on the front. Surprisingly there was only a shirt in the middle of the room, but I'm not complaining, I still get to keep my jeans for a little while longer.

Time moves differently here. I've walked around this small empty room numerous times. Eventually, I got tired of that and decided to start counting the tiles on the wall; once I hit 213 tiles, I stopped. Trying to keep myself occupied came as quite the challenge. I was fully out of ideas when the voice over the speaker echoed again. I was told that someone would be escorting me outside, soon. A few more minutes passed before anyone came to get me. I couldn't tell how long I was in the room, but it felt like hours. It was still light outside so I figured not much time could've passed at all.

I am left outside in the great heat. The sun's rays hit my face, and the humidity in the air immediately reached my entire body. I'm frozen in place as I stare around the courtyard. The area is large, as it goes on for miles on end. Whatever is visible to me, is surrounded by large barb-wired fences, ensuring that no one on this side can get out. Where I am in the courtyard gives me a perfect view of the place I had just been standing with my friends. They are no longer there, so a memory of our goodbye, is all that's left. I'm suddenly brought back to reality when I feel the guard that is escorting me outside, nudging my shoulder for me to continue walking.

As I am being escorted through the courtyard, I overhear some of the conversations between other people who are also being sent into the Bunker.

"My mom told me before I left, that her younger brother was taken to the Bunker. Maybe I'll get to meet him."

"I don't know, my parents kept telling me that no one stays in the Bunker too long. They freaked me out."

"Don't worry, I'm sure they won't hurt us down there."

"I hope you're right."

That one girl seems too hopeful, but for her sake, I really hope nothing bad happens down there. Many people are having similar conversations, where half are excited to go down, but the rest are concerned over some of the horror stories they have heard.

As I'm being led towards a row of buses, I see several kids from my high school. I've seen many of them walking through the hallways at school. Everyone's waiting to get onto the bus shares a similar facial expression, fear. The closer they get to the front of the line, the more worried they become. Their off-putting looks make me feel uneasy. Eventually, I am left in the back of the line for the very first bus. The line moves quickly, but once I get close enough to the front, I notice security scanning the names of each person as they get onto the bus. I imagine it's their way of keeping track of everyone who is heading into the Bunker.

I turn around and notice that no one else has lined up behind me, so when I take my step onto the bus the doors quickly shut behind me.

"Jeez."

"Keep walking forward," the security sounds stern and scans my name as I pass him. I make my way through the rows and see a single spot left open. It's in the back, next to a girl who looks oddly familiar. The bus starts moving before I can even sit down, so I stumble into the seat, I hope that no one saw that but the girl next to me lets out a soft chuckle under her breath.

I feel like a stalker as I keep glancing over at her, I'm still trying to place where I know her from. She inevitably catches me staring and decides to speak up.

"Can I help you?" She says it in a way that's inviting, not overly friendly but not too harsh, despite how weird I may look.

"Sorry," I completely shift my body so I am now facing her, "It's just you look so familiar, and I can't place where I know you from." I sound sympathetic, which puts a smile on her face.

"You were in Mrs. Walters' biology class, right?" I nod, "So was I."

I instantly remember her, "Right! You're Isabelle. You sat in the back with..." I'm blanking on her partner's name.

"Cooper." She adds.

"That's right. It was Cooper." I never really spoke to her while we were at school. We just ran in different friend groups, but it's a shame, she always seemed super friendly.

"So," I try to break the awkward silence, "What happened with your whole declaration?" Probably not the best opening line I could have come up with, it's a good thing she doesn't seem to mind.

"My boyfriend and I broke up a few months ago." Before I could even ask her to elaborate, she jumped right into telling me how it all went down.

"You're kidding. He cheated on you?" I'm appalled.

She starts laughing, "Yup, I caught him with some chick, when he was supposed to be 'studying.' But you want to hear the icing on the cake," I'm quick to nod "it turns out, she was his cousin that he never knew he had." That's what gets me. I am laughing my ass off; I nearly fall out of my seat.

"No fucking way! How'd you react to that?"

"I was shocked when I first caught them, but when he came knocking on my door to tell me he messed up, I didn't give him the time of day. He kept trying to explain what he did and accidentally spilled that she was his cousin. That's when I opened the door so he could see me laughing." Isabelle is now the one who is laughing uncontrollably. "The poor guy was in tears, but I just couldn't help myself." I was laughing so loud, that my mom walked downstairs and saw him crying in our doorway. He was so embarrassed that before she could say anything he ran down our driveway leaving me completely out of breath.

I've known this girl for maybe all of five minutes and I already feel a friendship forming. She is so uncontrollably funny, and she isn't even trying.

"When I was doing my declaration, I decided to ask them if they could tell me who my actual soulmate was." I cut her off "You can do that?" She nods and continues, "Turns out, he was my soulmate."

"Oh, you poor thing." I use my hand to cover the snickering.

"Trust me. I think I dodged a bullet."

"You're probably right. The last thing you'd want is to come home and find him sleeping with his sister."

She slaps the side of my arm, in hopes of trying to catch her breath. "That is disgusting." She folds over in tears when someone turns around to tell us to stop making so much noise. We both look at each other, and that brings on another fit of laughter.

The rest of the ride, we just go back and forth sharing stories. Turns out we have a lot in common. We like the same sort of music, we both love art and to top it all off, we both share a common hatred for Josie.

Who knew two people could be so alike? She told me that Josie made her first few high school years a living hell. She was the new kid, sophomore year, and accidentally sat in one of Josie's spots, within minutes, Josie made up some awful rumour about her and got the entire school thinking she was pregnant from two separate guys. I remember hearing about it, but never really cared, because it came from Josie, and it was just plain stupid.

At a moment's notice, the bus comes to a halt.

The guard at the front of the bus stands to make an announcement.

"When your name is called you will disembark without delay."

I look over to Isabelle and mock the guard's announcement, "When your name is called you will disembark without delay." He begins listing people off one by one. When he calls Isabelle's name she stands from her seat, and she gives me a quick hug, but before she lets go, she whispers in my ear.

"Before you get up, fix the piece of paper you have hiding in your bra." She lets go of me and begins walking towards the front. She glances back about halfway and gives me a slight smile.

When the guard looks away for a split second, I shift things in my shirt, so the paper isn't noticeable. I honestly forgot it was in there, but it must've been close to falling out if she noticed it. I'm so relieved that it was her who saw it because who knows what would've happened if it was someone else, or worse, one of the guards.

That's the moment I decided that if I was going to figure out a way out of the Bunker, I might as well get help from others who were inside with me, so I told myself to find her the second I had a chance. Nearly everyone has gotten off the bus. In no time, I'm the only person amongst the rows of empty seats. It takes the guard a while to come back after calling off the other people, so I decide to stand up and walk toward the front. To my surprise, the guard pops his head back into the bus and screams my name.

My ears are ringing, "Relax buddy, I'm right in front of you." The guard grabs my arm and drags me off the bus. "Hey," I slap his hands, "watch yourself."

When my feet hit the rubble of the ground beneath me, I am faced with an even bigger building. My neck is straining to see the top. It's hard to believe that this is the same building I had seen from the cliff only a few days ago. It looked much smaller, but then again, we were miles away.

Whenever I am with Spencer, all my problems seem to disappear. So, when I feel a rush of fear wash over me, I try to think back to those moments spent with him to calm myself down.

Up close it looks almost like a factory, but without all the smoke coming from the chimneys. The cool breeze that surrounds us picks up the dust from the ground, making it extremely hard to see. I squint my eyes to see the front of the building which looks almost normal. Something you would see walking down the main street, except this building has two large doors, reaching about midway up the wall; they are partly open. That's where I am being urged to go. When I walk through the doors, they immediately close almost catching on my hair, and the locks on the inside snap shut, preventing any of us from turning back around.

I look around the main room in hopes of seeing Isabelle or any familiar faces from my bus, but the room is empty, except for the guard and me. Even that doesn't last long, as I am now left by myself in this giant room, not knowing what to do. The walls are made of concrete, but they are painted an off-white type colour, chips of paint come flying off the wall as I drag my hand against it. This chill travels up my body when I hear a woman's voice come from behind me.

"Your group has already left my dear. What is your name so we can get this all sorted out?"

I look at her; looking her up and down. She is wearing a long-patterned skirt that passes her knees, a white buttoned-up blouse, and a large red belt joining the two at the seam. Sadie would lose her mind if she saw this outfit, even for me this looks bad. She has a pair of glasses, that she moves to the top of her head, where her hair is slicked back into a low bun. Something about her seems familiar, almost like I've seen her before. She coughs as if to say I am taking too long to come up with an answer.

"Kayleigh."

"Kayleigh?" She pauses for a second, "Why yes, you must be Kayleigh Harris." I nod in agreement, slightly concerned that she knows who I am but also relieved at the same time because maybe her knowing who I am is a good sign.

"We have been expecting you." She takes a few steps in my direction, "You have been on our radar for quite some time now. I'm Regina Storm, executive director. I make sure things run smoothly around here." I must have a look of uneasiness plastered on my face. "Don't worry dear, we will take great care of you. Now follow me, I will show you to your room."

I reluctantly follow her, something about that woman seems strange but I cannot put my finger on it quite yet.

She leads me down several hallways, with each turn the halls get darker, cobwebs line the walls, and the lights overhead flicker with every step. So far, the Bunker does not look like a five-star vacation spot. I try my best to remember as much as I can, but there are many twists and turns.

We pass by what she calls the eating quarters. As I pass by, I see a handful of people sitting at each table. None of them are conversing with each other, and all of them are eating quite robotically. I notice a few people from my bus. I stop in my tracks to peek my head into the room. Each one lifts their fork at the same time, not a single person is out of sync. I look visibly confused, but Regina reassures me that everything is alright, and I will be joining them very soon. After walking down a few more corridors, we arrive at my room. Regina opens the door with a key, and once it swings open, I can see a few sets of bunk beds, a toilet and sinks in the back right corner.

"I will leave you to make yourself comfortable." She closes the
door and walks away. After I know she is out of earshot I try to
open the door, but it is keycard operated, I have no choice but
to stay in my room.

No one else is in here, which gives the room an
ominous feeling. The beds are empty, and the room is spotless.
Had I not walked down the hallways, I never would've guessed
I was in the same place. I go over to the bunk that has my name
on it and rummage through the chest at the foot of the bed.
There are a couple of shirts and some pants. There is a
toothbrush, and some shower necessities, and right at the
bottom is a notebook with a pen. I take this opportunity to slip
the paper Kate had given me into the bottom of the chest. I try
my best to hide it in all the clothing, so even if the room is
covered with cameras, it would still be hidden. I take a second
to look around the room. It is quite spacious but extremely
plain. There is a clock sitting above the door, while everything
else in the room looks the same. The same sheets cover the
bunk beds, and the same chest lays at the foot of every bed.
Almost everything is a copy-paste of the thing directly next to
it. The only thing that differs from one bed to another is the
name that appears on the chest. I make my way around the
room in hopes of seeing a familiar name. To my surprise, every
name was familiar. These were the girls who had just been

called off my bus, I desperately searched for the one name that mattered, Isabelle. Her bed is directly across from mine, and both of us were assigned the top bunk.

This must be a sign, right? Maybe the two of us could figure out a plan together to get out of here. But she and the rest of my roommates have yet to find their way to the room. I can't help but wonder why I'm already here when the rest of my bus is nowhere in sight.

I make my way back to my bed and grab the note I had slipped in there earlier. It's not until now do I realize I have yet to open it. I start to unfold it layer by layer. Quickly unveiling a map. I spend the next few hours studying the map. I take the pen that was in my chest and start writing down everything I can remember from the walk I took with Regina. I make notes of where the eating quarters are, and how many turns it took to get from there to my room. I follow the lines of the map until I reach a point that has three stars drawn around it. It's printed onto the paper, so it couldn't be Kate who drew them.

The door of my room quickly opens, and one of the girls comes strolling in, I drop everything and hop off the top of my bed to go over to her.

"Hey," She doesn't acknowledge me at all. I run up in front of her and try saying hi again but her eyes pierce through my skin as she walks off past me. She climbs into her bed, without hesitation. Maybe this girl isn't big on talking, so I try not to think much of it. When more girls start walking in, I begin to get annoyed. Not one of them acknowledges me standing there. I try getting their attention, but it's like they can't hear me. Almost every single girl has come back to the room, except one.

Isabelle.

It's not for another hour, until the door opens for a final time tonight, and Isabelle strolls on in.

When I look at her, I realize that it is not the same girl I had just been conversing with on the bus ride over.

"Isabelle?" I call out her name but no answer.

"Isabelle?" I try again, and again until I decide to walk over to her and tap her on the shoulder.

"Isabelle? What is the matter with you?" She turns towards me, and her eyes are glazed over. All the life has been sucked out of them. I stumble backwards at the mere sight of her. I try regaining my balance before trying to snap her out of whatever trance she is in. "Holy shit, Isabelle. What happened to you?" Her eyes are piercing through my skin. She is not even acknowledging that I am standing in front of her. Seeing Isabelle like this, is heartbreaking. When the first few walked into the room, I hoped it was just their character, but seeing the complete change in character, something must've happened to them. Like all the other girls, Isabelle manages to walk over to her assigned bed without thinking twice. I walk up towards every other girl in the room, wondering if any of them has snapped out of whatever trance they are in, but they all have the same look in their eyes.

Darkness.

I can't begin to express what the sight of these girls is doing to me. Seeing them like this makes me feel like I'm sharing a room with robots. When they look in my direction, they aren't looking at me but through me. Every time I make eye contact with one of them, I feel a shiver run up my spine. My mind is running wild, thinking of all the ways this could've happened to them. *Regina had something to do with this, right? But how come I'm not acting this way? Whatever it is that's going on here, I need to figure it out. Fast.*

I headed back towards my bed to grab the paper I had been studying before everyone walked in. I spent the rest of my time analyzing the map. I look it over so many times that I can start to picture myself walking through it. I have spent so much time looking over this map, that I don't even realize the time. When I finally look up by the door, I can see the clock strike 11:00 pm. Looking around the room, I notice everyone is sleeping in their respective beds. I'm not sure how long they've been like this. I'm about to put the map down, but I notice

writing in the bottom corner of the page. I can barely make out
what is written on the corner of the paper.

M.C.

M.C.? What could M.C. be? I assume it's somebody's
name. When my friends and I were looking up information
about the Bunker, we came across lists of names of people who
had been sent down to the Bunker. There were thousands of
names, over the years, so I try running through as many names
as I can remember, trying to see where M.C. fits in.

After thinking for some time, a light bulb in my head
goes off and I only remember one possibility that could work.
But it's not a name I had read on a paper but one from a story
Spencer had told me.

Mason Clark.

The only person to ever escape the Bunker. Spencer
had been telling me about this guy the night we were on the
cliff. He said he hadn't known much about him but knew the
government was keeping anything involving him, under wraps.
M.C. must be him. That's the only thing that would make
sense. A map of the Bunker, with initials on it? *Definitely him.*
Potentially having figured out the first step in getting out of
here is bittersweet. If I can solve this, then there is a chance I
could do this on my own. But if it weren't for Spencer, I never

would've known that there even was a chance of getting out of here. I miss him.

A guy has never affected me as much as Spencer Brown has in such a short period of time. I know it's bad to say, but I really wish he were here. If he were here, then we could solve this together, but if he were here that would also mean that Josie was never his soulmate, and I think that's what I'm secretly hoping for the most.

Thinking about Spencer makes me emotional, so I decide to slip the map under my pillow, so I can get some sleep. Just as I am about to close my eyes the door to our room swings open.

I jolt up in my bed at the sound of it, but there is no reaction from any of the girls. They are as still as statues, fast asleep. This tall broad man, covered with tattoos, walks in. He touches the side of his ear. It looks like a communicating device that is connected by a wire that is attached at the waist of his pants. He is wearing black plastic gloves and has his hand on a gun on the side of his hip. I pray to myself that whatever it is he is doing here has nothing to do with me. With my luck, he stops right in front of my bed and shines a flashlight in my face.

"Kayleigh Harris, please follow me." When I don't immediately move, he says it again, but with more conviction.

This time I don't hesitate. I hop off the top bunk and follow directly behind him nipping at his heels.

We've already walked down what feels like twenty different hallways and I ask him where he is taking me.

"No talking." He snaps, not even looking in my direction.

"Jeez, I was only asking."

"I said no talking." This time he turns around to face me.

"Someone seriously woke up on the wrong side of the bed. But fine, no talking" I seal my lips and pretend to throw away a key. Damn. Not even a smirk crosses his face.

He turns back around and continues walking down the hall. Without warning he stops in front of a large glass door, leaving me to run into the back of his heels. He bends downwards to wipe off the dust I got on his shoes. When he gets back up, he is standing directly in front of me.

"Don't move." I wince at the smell of the coffee on his breath.

"Wouldn't dream of it." He leaves me outside the door, while he goes in. When he's far enough out of sight, I move. I'm walking up and down the hallway that he left me in looking for anything out of the ordinary. Everything here is cleaner, there's no dust on the floor, no paint chips flying off the wall, it's just, clean. The floor isn't concrete, but wood, and the lights aren't flickering. If I hadn't walked all the way here, I would've guessed that the grumpy guard kidnapped me.

The glass door springs back open, and the broad man comes back out.

"I thought I told you not to move."

"You did, but I chose not to listen." He rolls his eyes at me and motions for me to follow him down the hallway.

At the end of the hallway, there are these sliding doors that open once we get close. The guard stands to the side and allows me to enter first. When I step inside, I realize I am standing in what looks like a doctor's office. There is a table in the middle of the room, and medical devices that are lining the wall.

"Sit on the table and wait for the doctor."

"What am I doing here?"

"No questions. Just do what I say."

"Come on man, you know that's not going to happen."

"Just sit down."

I roll my eyes and attempt to jump up onto the table. After failing a few times, I stood leaning up against it staring at the guard. With a grunt, he walks over to me and lifts me onto the table.

"Watch where your hands go next time bud."

He shakes his head and storms out of the room.

"Thanks."

I'm now alone in this room, and it's honestly freaking me out. It's not the idea of being in the doctor's office, but the idea that I'm the patient. That's why I liked working at the clinic, I was the one in control, and I got to make the animals feel better. Being on this side of it just feels wrong.

Before I spiral even further, the glass door opens revealing someone walking in wearing a white coat with their face covered with a mask. All I can see are their eyes. They're dark and mysterious, not comforting at all. My nerves come rushing back in, as the figure moves directly in front of me.

"Um, maybe you can explain why I'm here?" There is no response coming from the doctor, not even a nod of his head. He stands very still, like a statue, his eyes never wandering elsewhere.

The doctor starts moving around the room in search of something. He opens several drawers, shuffling things around. When he returns to his position in front of me, I can see this long needle filled with a serum placed in his right hand.

Immediately, stress starts to build inside of me. "What is that?"

The doctor gives me no answer as I am squirming in my seat. The closer he gets to me, the quicker my heart starts to beat. I shoot my hands up in the air, "No way, you are not putting that needle in me without telling me what's in it." He keeps moving closer and closer to me, despite my pleas. In one continuous motion, the doctor grabs ahold of my arm and injects me with the contents of the needle. Once, he removes the needle from my arm, the doctor exits the room without saying a word. As he walks away, I yell after him, "What the fuck?"

My arm feels heavy, and with every passing second, I'm finding it harder and harder to stay awake. I keep my eyes open for as long as I possibly can. Right before my eyes shut, I hear the door opening again. I see the guard who had brought me here standing in the corner with a grin on his face, as my eyes finally close.

My eyes open and I can tell that I am still in the same room as before, but my arms and legs are secured to the table. I have no way of moving from my spot. I squint as the bright white light fills the room. Something about being here feels different. I'm no longer anxious, and I have no recollection of how it is I got to this point. At this moment, all I know is that this is where I am supposed to be.

Seconds later I feel the restraints loosen and I am no longer attached to the table. I slide off with ease, immediately exiting the bright room, and heading straight for my bunk. My body knows the way, like I've done this walk thousands of times. Taking each turn with conviction, I've fully let my body control me. My thoughts and my motions are no longer in sync I still have full awareness of where I am, but regardless of what I am thinking, my body will only do what it wants to do. I feel almost like a puppet, but I don't know who my master is.

The feeling is strange, like I'm in a constant state of uncertainty. When I reopened my eyes in the bright lights, I felt like I was being reborn. Anything from before that moment is lost. Any memory I had from before I woke up is now gone.

I'm still walking through the halls, making turns I've never made before, but my body never slows down. I'm walking with determination. This other voice in my head is giving me instructions on where to go, and when I need to be there. Although I have a sense that this voice is not mine, I have no control over what I am doing and obey everything they say. The voice tells me to move faster. To get to my room, as soon as possible. My feet just aren't moving quickly enough. Before I know it, I'm nearly running through the halls, with the feeling that nothing will get in my way.

Until something gets in my way and makes me stop. The voice in my head is getting louder by the second, my hands shoot up for my ears to block out the noise, but the voice won't stop. The lights overhead are flickering. Each time the light flickers the voice gets louder. They are going back and forth with each other, increasing the suspense that is running through my body, but I am at a standstill. The walls around me get smaller and smaller as the voice gets louder and louder. My legs are burning up, urging for motion, but something is preventing me from moving.

A tap on my shoulder jolts me around. The voice inside my head grows desperate, but with every spoken word the voice gets lower and lower until all the commands are over. A new, soft, and endearing voice takes the place of the old devilish one.

"Kayleigh?"

All it took was my name.

I instantly snap back to my old self; everything comes rushing back to me. The doctor's room, the needle, the guard, my fear, being strapped down onto a table, the loss of control I had over my body, the map I have hidden under my pillow, Isabelle, the girls, Regina Storm. Everything came back to me the second he said my name.

I nearly lose my balance, but his arms wrap around my waist to grab hold of me. I look up at him, admiring the way he looks, and feels. I pray that this is not some trick my mind is playing on me and that he truly is here. But how could he be standing in front of me? How did he get here? Why is he here?

All these questions are running through my mind, and I know he can tell. He squeezes me tighter, holding me for only a few seconds. That's all it takes for me to feel safe. I allow myself to sink into his arms. This is the moment I've been thinking of, since the first time he called me Satan. I never want this feeling to end, he can hold onto me forever and I will not complain, but I know that can't happen.

I remember everything, and it doesn't take a genius to figure out that whatever type of place Regina is running, is no longer safe for us. If they think they have me under their control, that's how it's going to be. Once they know I've snapped back to reality, who knows what they could do to me next? I push his arms to his sides and look up into his eyes. I'm trying to formulate my thoughts and how I am going to tell him all of this without either of us getting caught. He looks so innocent now, having no idea what this place has in store. I feel like a terrible person for having to break this news to him, but he needs to know what we are up against. This feeling of needing to protect him from all of this is strong, but from what I've discovered from him this past year, he is tougher than what people assume; he can handle whatever comes his way.

That said, escaping the Bunker has become ten times more complicated. Instead of only having to worry about myself, I now have Spencer to worry about too. Having him here may have been the best thing that could've happened though.

We are two people who work well together, and hopefully in the end that's what gets us out of here.

If it weren't for him, I could've still been controlled by the Bunker, but Spencer Brown just saved my life. Now I will do whatever it takes to save his.

Chapter 22

SPENCER

"Spencer?" Her voice is frail, but the same as I remember. She lowers my arms as she takes a step away from me. I look at her amazed. I was walking with a group of kids when I saw her racing through the halls. I have so much to tell her. Like how they split up the guys and the girls when getting off the bus. I was the last one off the bus, and after waiting twenty minutes, that's when I finally decided to hop off. I walked through the doors, and everyone was already gone, but I somehow managed to find my way back to them. That's when

I realized how strange everyone was acting. Almost like they were puppets.

When I saw Kayleigh, I called out to her multiple times, but when I wasn't getting a reaction from her, I left my group. I wasn't prepared to have found her so quickly but I'm glad I did.

I go to wrap my arms around her again, but she pushes my arms away and grabbed ahold of my wrist. I look up at her confused. She gives me zero reassurance and starts dragging me down the halls. It feels like we are running in circles, and Kayleigh is getting more visibly annoyed with every wrong turn.

"We've been down this hallway four times."

"Thank you, Spencer, I couldn't tell."

"I'm just trying to help."

"Well, you're not. So just stop talking."

"But…"

She looks back at me with daggers. I immediately stopped talking. After running around the halls countless more times, I can't help but smirk towards Kayleigh.

"What?"

I look at her silently, with my shoulders shrugged.

"You can speak now."

"Why don't we go down that way?" I point towards a hallway we have yet to travel down. Her eyes follow my finger and widen when she sees it.

"Why didn't you say something before?"

Before I could even get a word out, she was dragging me down this new hallway, this time knowing exactly where she was going. We finally reach a closed door; Kayleigh puts her hands up against the handle and hesitantly pushes against the door. She seems surprised when the door swings open easily. She drags me through the room, till we reach her bed, she quickly climbs on and sits cross-legged facing me.

"I have something super important to show you."

"Hold on, Satan, I don't think this is the first place you and I should be doing this." She looks at me confused.

"You know," I whisper, "sex?"

She slaps my arm, "Seriously Spencer, is that the only thing on your mind?"

I'm chuckling with a giant grin on my face, "Come on, I was only mostly joking." Kayleigh's face turns a bright red, leaving me to know that she is not completely opposed to the idea.

Kayleigh begins again but her breath is slightly ragged, but she quickly calms herself when I place my hands on her thighs.

She takes a while to start speaking again so I start, "You will not believe what I have to tell you." She listens to me talk about how I got into the Bunker. Grasping every word that comes out of my mouth. I'm telling her about waiting in line to get onto the bus, sitting in the back with some guy who was caught cheating, how everyone was called off the bus when I wasn't and being alone when I finally got into the building. I was expecting some sort of reaction out of Kayleigh, but she has full composure, she doesn't even seem surprised.

"Did you just hear what I said?"

She lifts her hand pointing out all the girls sleeping in their beds. I hadn't realized anyone else was in this room. *Does this mean she experienced the same things as me?* "Oh, shit."

"When you found me," she takes a deep breath before continuing, "I was acting that same way. I had no control over my body, and I couldn't do anything about it. I had these voices in my head telling me to get to my room. They were counting down, and I knew I didn't want them to get to zero. My body was just moving down the halls, but I had no control over it," I've never seen her look this freaked out before. "When I turned around towards you, everything came back to me. Where I was, what I was doing, everything. They injected something in me, Spencer." She looks at me with tears in her eyes, "I told them not to, I didn't want them to put anything in me. The feeling when I woke up in that state, was cold, dark, and alone. Everything was out of my control; it was like I was sleeping, and someone was using my body as a puppet." I reach out for her hand, and she gives it a tight squeeze.

I'm at a loss for words, nothing is making sense to me right now. I don't understand why Kayleigh was taken after everyone else. *If I hadn't gotten off the bus when I did, would the same thing have happened to me?* Why were all my roommates affected and I wasn't? Nothing is making any sense.

I wipe away some of the tears from her face. She looks up at me and asks, "Remember that name you told me about when we were talking on the cliff?" I think back to that night trying to remember the name she is referring to. When I look back at her with defeat in my eyes, she quickly fills in the blanks "you said his name was Mason Clark. Do you remember that?"

"Oh yeah. He was the guy who escaped the Bunker." She is nodding in agreement, to say that I am finally following her train of thought.

"Please tell me you remember something else about him." She sounds desperate.

I immediately regret shaking my head. She reaches behind her to grab her pillow. It almost looks like she is about to smack me with it, so I flinch.

"Relax, Jackass I wasn't going to hit you."

Instead, she reaches for a small folded-up piece of paper she had hiding under the pillow.

"What's this," she hands me the paper. I unfold it to see a map. "Is this a map of the Bunker?"

"Look at the initials at the bottom."

"M.C.? Mason Clark." I look up at her.

"That's what I'm hoping for."

"Where'd you even get this?"

"Kate gave it to me before I went inside. She said she found it on the decrypted file."

I fold it back up and hand it to her, she quickly places it back where she first got it from.

"I think, if the initials are for Mason Clark, then we can figure out a way out of here." She's waiting for me to answer, but I can't figure out what to say. "Spencer?" She waits, "You going to say something or just sit there, daydreaming about sex."

"First of all, I'm not always thinking about sex." She lifts her eyebrow at me. "Ok fine, maybe I was kind of daydreaming about sex, but I was also thinking that I may have another way out of here." She has a puzzled look on her face but seems open to hearing my idea. "The whole point of the bunker is to take those who haven't found their soulmate out of society, right?"

"Yeah?"

"Well, if we find our soulmate in the bunker then they'd have to release us!"

"I- I don't think that would work."

"Why not?"

"Well, last time I checked, neither one of us found our soulmate here..." For a super smart girl, she is taking forever to figure this one out. Something finally clicks in her head, and she starts throwing questions at me. "Wait, how are you even here? What happened to Josie? Is this even real?" She starts poking my body, I slap her hand away.

"Long story short, turns out Josie was the evil conniving bitch you said she was and was never actually my soulmate." I let that sit for a few seconds before the realization finally hit her. "Oh my god," she slaps the side of my arm, and it stings, "are you, my soulmate?" I rub my arm and cup her mouth in one swift motion. She is screaming so loud she might wake the whole building.

"Took you long enough to figure it out, Satan. Now can I move my hand or are going to keep screaming?"

She nods her head and I move my hand away from her mouth.

I so desperately want to kiss her; she is sitting so close to me it would be too easy. Her lips caressing mine would solve so many of our problems. All I need to do is grab her face. But I can't, not right now.

"Spencer," hearing my name come out of her mouth shoots butterflies through my body, "I'm not sure going to someone is a great idea."

"Why not? Maybe they'll let us go?"

"Considering they think I'm under some 'serum,' I doubt they're going to let us go."

"I can always go to someone and ask what would happen if we were to find our soulmate inside the Bunker?"

"I mean that could work, but I'm still not sold on it. If you decide to do that, just don't accidentally tell them, I have control over my body again."

"I promise. I'd never do anything to put you in danger."

"Ok fine." She leans forward and gives me what I have been so desperately waiting for since I found her. We both sink into the kiss, but she ends it quickly. "You must go before someone comes. I'll try to figure out more of the map, and I'll come find you."

I slowly step down from the top bunk but before I can head toward the door, she peers over the side.

"This guy you sat next to; did he mention who he cheated with?"

"He did. Why?"

"Please tell me it was his cousin."

"No way you just guessed that. How'd you know?" She has a grin spread across her face and looks toward the bunk bed directly in front of her.

"Don't worry about it. Now get out of here before someone sees you."

I rush towards the door but look back before I head out. "You have to tell me how you knew." She waves to me before I slip out the door and start making my way back through the halls. I walk for a while before I finally find my room. I had already passed by it when I was following my group; it just took me some time to re-orient myself after running through these halls with Kayleigh.

...

It feels like the middle of the night when the door bursts open. I am the only one to wake up from the disturbance, as two armed guards make their way through the room until they reach the front of my bed.

"Spencer Brown? Your presence has been requested."

I try asking them by whom, but they refuse to give me an answer. They also never give me a chance to get down from my bed, they just yank me off and start dragging me through the corridor until I regain control of my feet. I walk down the hallways for the third time tonight but this time with two guards at either side of me. Having done this several times tonight, I am starting to remember my way around part of this place.

I'm stopped in front of this large archway leading down a narrow hallway. I am reluctant at first but one of the guards shoves me from the back and I start marching down the narrow path until I reach a door with a bell. He slaps the back of my head when I stand staring at the door for too long. I rub the back of my head and turn to face the guard. Before I can get a word out, he grunts and motions towards the bell. I reach to ring the bell and the door swings open.

The room is quite large and more open than what our rooms look like. The walls are designed with a marble pattern, one that is similar to the kitchen in Josie's house. They are lined with bookshelves and the room has a giant desk right in the center. There is a chair that faces the back wall with a window that overlooks the loading bay, where all the buses go. When I make my presence known, the chair twirls around to portray a lady in her late twenties maybe thirties, wearing glasses far too large for her face. At first, I panic at the sight of her, as she reminds me of someone I once knew, but the sound of her voice brings me back to the present moment.

"You must be Spencer. I have heard lots about you."

I walk towards her and extend my hand. Might as well get people to like me. "Nice to meet you Mrs....?" I wait for her to fill in the blank.

"Mrs. Storm. But why be so formal, call me Regina."

"Okay, Regina. I assume you needed me for something, given the fact I was fetched for in the middle of the night."

"Why yes, I apologize for the late-night rendezvous, but I was informed that you missed your doctor's appointment when you first came in today. I wanted to see why that was."

"That was my mistake, I got separated from the group so I figured I would head back towards my room and wait for them to return. It took me a while to find my room. I got all turned around walking down some of the halls."

"Makes sense, some of these halls can be quite the maze." Regina has this devilish grin, that makes me very uneasy.

To ease the tension I ask, "If you don't mind me asking, are you the person in charge here?"

"I am one of the tops, yes."

"Great. I was hoping to discuss something with you then." She seemed confused but invited me to sit in a chair that was directly across from her desk.

"What were you looking to discuss."

"Well, I was wondering what would happen if someone inside the Bunker were to find their soulmate. Would it be possible to leave at that point?"

She moves her glasses from her face and places her palms together on the desk. "I wish that were possible Spencer, I do," *I can feel a but coming,* "but I'm afraid it's just not possible to find your soulmate down here."

"And why's that?" I look puzzled.

"There are two separate facilities for the men and women." *Why is she lying to me?* "With that being said, no one would be able to make actual physical contact with their soulmate." My mind flashes back to the kiss I just shared with Kayleigh. Unless I was dreaming, I am certain I made physical contact with her.

"Is that so?"

"I'm afraid it is. Now, if that was what you needed to discuss, I would have one of my associates escort you back to your room. The doctor left many hours ago, so we will have you checked out in the morning. It was a pleasure meeting you, Spencer. Hopefully, we will see each other again sometime."

"Same here." I step back into the hallway and am faced with another guard. *How many guards do they have in this place?* He escorts me back toward my room and shoves me through the door. I somewhat memorized the way back to my room from Regina's office.

When the door shuts behind me, I try to pry it open, but the door has already locked. I slam my fist onto the side of the door when it doesn't budge. *I need to get out of here and talk to Kayleigh.* The door must only be locked because I still have control. If Kayleigh's door was unlocked, when everyone is supposed to be "under," then that means after their doctor's visit, I'll probably be in the same state as my roommates.

I'm still thinking about what Regina said about not being able to make physical contact with your soulmate. Something big is going on here because unless I magically moved between two different facilities or was fantasizing about that kiss, I can promise you that the girls are right next door. Regina Storm, *who still looks extremely familiar,* is keeping secrets from all of us. I thank myself that I never mentioned Kayleigh because I'm not sure what would have happened if they found out that we saw each other.

From this point on, I am only going to trust Kayleigh, but maybe if I play my cards correctly, Regina may begin to trust me. I don't think anyone else here truly knows what is going on besides her. I really hope Kayleigh figures something out quickly, and hopefully she finds me fast. I have a bad feeling that after the doctor's visit, I'm going to be in the same state as all the other people here.

Chapter 23

Kayleigh

"Fuck!" I scream into my pillow, as I am beyond frustrated right now. I have been looking at this goddamn piece of paper all night long, and I haven't been able to figure out anything. I was able to map out the places Spencer and I had walked through last night and where the eating quarters were, but not much else. The lines on the map are confusing, and they lead in every which way. I'm hoping by the end of the day I will be able to map out a few more places. There's one spot on the map that I need to find. It has a couple of stars written around it. Once I figure out where it is, I can figure out what it means.

I've been awake for a few hours now; I never really went to bed. I tried waking a few of the girls, thinking that maybe the way they were acting was a first-day thing, but none of them woke up. Sitting in my bed for hours, I decided that today would be a day that I would try and blend in. Try acting like all the other girls, so no one suspects a thing. This way I can try to locate Spencer without too many people keeping an eye on me.

I had reached the point where I had just been staring at the clock waiting for anything to happen. When the hand strikes exactly 9:00 a.m., everyone shoots awake from their bed. The sudden movements scare me shitless. The girls all move around the room in a robotic style, as they rush to get ready. I do my best to follow their lead, as they navigate through the room, finding anything they might need. Eventually, we all end up dressed in matching uniforms. When the clock strikes 9:30 a.m. the doors swing open and a single guard comes waltzing in, to take us to the eating quarters. We march in a line, and when we arrive, we make our way to a long table in the back, and everyone takes their respective seat.

There are piles of food laid out in front of us and I am about to start digging in when I notice no one else is moving.

Not even a muscle, they stay still in their seats staring in a single direction. I restrain myself from reaching for the food until everyone else starts eating. More and more people fill the room, and still, no one is eating. *Maybe we can only start when everyone is here?* I try to subtlety look around the room, two guards are standing at every door, and there are three doors visible to me. That means six guards in total.

From studying the map last night, I know there are only three doors in this room, so the room with the stars isn't here.

I lose my train of thought when I see the main doors open again. There is one more table that has yet to be filled, and a line of boys comes marching through the door. When they take their seats, everyone begins eating. I was expecting Spencer to be with the last group, but I still haven't seen him. I get this feeling of panic coursing through my veins until I hear the door open one more time. The doctor who I vaguely remember comes walking in with someone following him at his heels.

It's him.

His hair is swaying with every step he takes. I had just seen him yesterday but the sheer sight of him makes me soft inside. His head jerks my way, and I try to show him a soft smile, but he isn't the Spencer I was just talking with. Something has changed. I'm far away but I can tell that his gorgeous green eyes aren't his anymore. The same look that fills Isabell's eyes is taking over his.

I know how to fix him, but I need to get close. I won't be able to get close enough right now without alarming all the guards in the room, so I have to wait. Everyone around me starts reaching for food. Hopefully, Spencer can wait a little bit before I snap him out of whatever trance they put him in. Today I need to focus on placing more things on the map and blending in. My only chance of doing so is if I stay clear of the guard's radar. Spencer's going to have to be okay until I can get to him.

SPENCER

EARLIER

My bed shakes, and I have these two bright lights shining in my eyes. Two figures are standing by my bed with flashlights facing me. They instruct me to get dressed and follow them out of the room. I peer up at the clock and notice that it is only half past four. I'm barely awake when they drag me down the halls.

"Why do you always have to drag me down the halls?"

"Shut up and keep moving."

"Noted."

They leave me in front of yet another narrow hallway. I groggily make my way down it, until I reach a sliding door. I walk through it and see a makeshift doctor's office, with a table directly in the middle and medical devices lining the wall. I'm told to take a seat at the table, and that the doctor will be with me in just a moment.

I know what's going to happen if I stay here, Kayleigh told me this is what happened to her. I'm still half asleep but adrenaline immediately kicks in, I need to get out of this room before they inject me. I spring off the table and walk towards the door, but it won't slide open or even budge. I try banging and screaming for someone to open the door, but nothing changes.

I turn back around and notice a mirror in front of the table, it's hard to tell whether it's a two-way or not, so I start banging on it. I hope that someone may be watching on the other side. But who am I kidding, no one is going to let me out of here, even if someone is watching.

Moments pass by until the door opens again, and two people come strolling in. One person who is wearing all white, with a mask, and another person who has no shame in being known.

"Why are you here?"

"I told you, Spencer, we would be seeing each other very soon."

"I get that, but why are we in a doctor's office at 4:30 in the morning."

"The check-up usually takes a few hours, so I wanted to ensure you had plenty of time to make breakfast in the morning." She is making her way around the room, "I also wanted to take this opportunity to discuss a few matters with you."

I walk towards the side wall and lean up against it with my arms crossed in front of my body.

"What matters were you looking to discuss?"

"I've read your file several times, you were captain of the baseball team, one of the most popular guys in school, and you had a volunteer position at a veterinarian clinic…"

"Thank you very much for listing off my accomplishments, but what difference does that make down here?"

"The reason why I am listing all these accomplishments, smart ass, is because you have the perfect criteria for a bigger job down here."

"What's that supposed to mean?"

"I want you to agree to a job that works directly with me."

"You know, I am truly honoured Regina, but what would that entail."

"You would start as one of the guards, and eventually work your way up to working directly under me. You will be moved out of your room for something more private and..."

I cut her off, "I was actually meaning to ask you about why all my roommates are acting so weird."

"Weird? What do you mean?" She looks disappointed when I bring this up.

"Well, I've noticed that ever since I split up with them yesterday, no one has been the same," I have to be careful with what I say, so she doesn't seem suspicious, "None of them talk anymore, and they all move like robots."

"Well, Spencer, the reason for that is because none of them had the same potential as you. Any other concerns you may have?"

"Since you asked, I was hoping you could explain to me why I saw a group of girls, yesterday while I was wandering around." *Shut up.* "You mentioned that there were two facilities, but I'm positive that I did not move between facilities." *Spencer you idiot, why would you say something?*

"Oh, Spencer. I wish you didn't say that. Is that why you asked me about finding your soulmate yesterday?" She snaps her fingers in the direction of the doctor, who slowly makes his way toward me.

"What are you doing?" I put my arms up in front of me to prevent the doctor from getting closer.

"It seems to me that you may not have the qualities we are looking for in the end."

"You don't need to do this." The doctor is making his way closer and closer, with a needle in his right hand. "Wait please."

"You're running out of time Spencer; you better ask quickly."

"Why do you look so familiar? Ever since I saw you, I couldn't bear the thought of knowing you from somewhere." She smiles at that question, but before she can answer me, I look down to see the contents of the needle dispensing into my arm.

I feel my eyes beginning to close and my last thought was of Kayleigh. Hopefully, she finds me soon enough.

Chapter 24

Kayleigh

Breakfast finishes about sixty minutes after everyone starts eating. A loud bell rings over several hidden speakers, and everyone stands up in unison, leaving everything on the tables exactly as is. At this point, I've noticed half a dozen new guards entering the room. Each guard, gun in hand, marches over to a designated table leading the group of kids out into the hallway. Given that we are in the far corner of the eating quarters, we are the final table after Spencer's group to head out.

When we step out into the hallway, I feel a cool breeze wash over me. We march in unison one behind the other, as we make our way down each corridor. Additional guards are lined against the wall, ensuring no one steps out of line.

I am stuck in the middle of my group, and as I look out in front of me, I can barely see Isabelle's hair sway, as she is up in front directly behind the leading guard. We keep in stride for a little while longer until everyone comes to an abrupt halt. I stumble into the person in front of me causing a domino effect. As I see each girl, stumble into the person in front of them, I pray that Isabelle doesn't move.

I'm trying to mentally communicate with my friend, but my fear becomes a reality when she stumbles into the back of the guard. He quickly spins around. He gives Isabelle a look over and waves down one of the guards standing by the other wall just up ahead. Once they reach our line, the guard that she bumped into points to Isabelle, and she is immediately taken out of the line into the open hallway. She is completely defenseless as two giant guards surround her. They both have this devilish smile appear on their face before they lead her into a nearby room.

It takes everything in me to not jump out of line and run to her defense. It feels like an eternity before they return. Her face drips with blood, and her right eye is barely kept open.

Every possible thing that could've happened to her starts
running through my head, and tear begins to roll down my face.
It's sickening to think that they can do whatever they please,
with no repercussions. My only hope right now is that Isabelle
cannot remember what happened to her, or that she didn't feel
any pain. If I wasn't already completely determined to get out
of this shithole before, I am now. This is why I need to find a
way out of here, I can't keep letting this happen to defenseless
people.

When she gets brought back into the line, we
immediately continue marching. We spend what feels like
another ten minutes making our way through the halls before
we reach a secluded corner out of view from other halls. When
the door gets pushed open a puff of steam spews out. All the
other groups have already made their way into the working
area, the only benches that remain open are those that are
designated for my group. When the last of us enter the room,
the door shuts behind us. Each person is tasked with a specific
section of the workhouse, and no one moves from their spot
once they get settled. I make my way towards the only open
spot, assuming that's where I am supposed to be. We are thirty
people or so working, but I have no idea what it is we are
working on.

There are rows of buttons on my desk, and every so often one would light up. It did not take me long to figure out that I needed to press the button once it lit up. If I was too slow in pressing the button, a piercing alarm would start ringing. That's my entire job down here, pressing a button when it lights up. *What was the point of going to school, if all I have to do is press a fucking button? This makes me feel incompetent.* It's offensive to think that this is what life has come to. All these people could have had real potential in doing something for society that truly matters, but instead, we were all taken here, to spend the rest of our lives doing repetitive tasks that are fucking useless.

Sitting at a desk and pressing a button gets boring after a while, so I decided to count the minutes between every time I click the button. *1, 2, 3, 4*... as I count, my eyes wander the room, I'm looking at every person robotically working at their desk. *60, 61, 62, 63*... When I spot Isabelle, I can see the remnants of the dry blood smeared across her face. Her eye is swollen, and she looks like a mess. All I want to do is see if she's okay, but I can't put myself in danger just yet. *101, 102, 103, 104*... No one else in this room looks like Isabelle, no one has cuts on their face, or blood dripping onto their clothes. I feel terrible that I'm the reason this happened to her. *222, 223, 224, 225*... Speaking of the guards, I have not seen them in the room at all, since we've been here. It somewhat surprised me but having been here for what feels like forever, I can tell you that I am covered in sweat and smell like rotten eggs. No one would voluntarily stand in here, for long periods of time. *296, 297, 298, 299...* The light flickers again. 300 seconds between each time the button lights up, that's 5 minutes total.

My eyes are starting to feel heavy. I have no idea how long it's been since we've been down here, but it is getting harder to stay alert. Just as my eyes are about the shut, I hear the large metal door swing open, crashing against the inner wall. A lone guard marches in and walks towards one of the workers. They tap his shoulder three times, and the worker jumps from his seat and follows the guard out the open door, leaving the station unmanned. The metal door slams behind them. In the time that it takes for the guard and the worker to return, I have clicked my button three times. When the worker walks in, I study his face. Thankfully I see no cuts or bruises, which means, they didn't take him out to beat him. When the worker finds his seat again, the guard taps out the very next person to the first worker's right. It takes them another 15 minutes to return. I let this go on with a few more people until it's safe to say that, in the 15 minutes that they are gone, no guard is in the vicinity of the workshop. Like clockwork, the guard waltzes back in and taps the next person out.

I've established a plan, now that I know I have 15 minutes to do anything in here. On the map, there were stars drawn next to a room, insinuating that, that's where the passage out of here is. Based on the design of the map, and the number of hallways leading from the eating quarters to here, I can only assume that the passage would be from this room. I've already wasted most of my time making sure that the guard returns every 15 minutes. By the time I decide that I will search this room, only a handful of workers are left to be taken out.

When the worker that is two spots down from me is taken out of the room, I spring into action, searching every inch of the space around me. I decided not to push my luck in searching the first time. I am sitting in my spot several minutes prior to the guard returning. When he takes out the person directly next to me, I test my luck even more. I just make it back to my spot with enough time to press my button. When the guard returns, he watches the girl next to me sit down and taps my shoulder three times. I stand up from my chair and follow him out the door. I jump slightly when the door slams behind me, luckily the guard is several feet in front of me, and he does not notice. I manage to catch up and I follow directly behind him as we head down some more narrow hallways until he forces me through another archway. I was somewhat expecting another doctor's visit or a meeting with Storm, but instead, he brought me to a bathroom. *At least they allow us to do that, right?* I was reluctant at first when the guard showed no sign of leaving, but once I realized that I was not supposed to be in control of my thoughts, I did what I needed and hurried back to the workshop.

There's only a handful of people left for the guard to take out. I know I won't have time to search the entire room in one day, so I do what I can thoroughly, and decide to search more tomorrow. I've pulled back curtains, and crawled under desks, searching for any possible spot that a hidden passage could be. I've managed to search and research the area around my station and my neighbor's station. It was difficult getting around some of the people as they were hard to move out of the way, so in a few scenarios, I had to squeeze in between people to properly search their area. I can confidently say that the passage is nowhere near me.

When I get back to my spot, I look over to the far end of the room. I see him standing there, staring into the distance, completing his tasks one after another. Watching him mindlessly work, tugs at my emotions. I remember how happy he was when we would work together in the clinic, or the conversations we would have in biology class. All I want to do is free him from this because from what I remember, the constant voice in my head telling me what to do is tiring. I only had to deal with it for maybe a few hours, but he's been dealing with it all day. But I know I can't risk him drawing more attention to our situation before I figure out where exactly this passage is.

When the guard comes back with the last worker, he is accompanied by three other people in uniform. *It's a little much, considering they are dealing with people who have zero control over their actions.* But row by row they are escorting all of us back to our rooms. My group is the last to be escorted back as we wait in line by the door.

Walking in the hallway that is filled with flickering bright lights, gives my eyes a shock after working in the dimmed room for hours. The only noise you can hear while walking around is the sound of feet marching in unison. We all smell of steam, and many of us have dirt all over our clothes. The walk back to our room is short, it is only four turns down separate hallways. We went left, then right twice, and left one more time, until we reached the giant door that had become all too familiar.

I clean myself up, by taking off my uniform and hopping into a fast shower. There is no such thing as privacy in the place, so everyone showers in the same room. It feels like a boy's locker room, but it could be worse, at least we are only girls here, and no guards are watching us.

Once I get all the dirt off me, I throw on the single set of pajamas that they give us and climb into my bed. I go to pull out the hidden map from under my pillow praying that no one else found it. I thank my lucky stars that it's still there. I had this weird feeling that people come and rummage through our room when we weren't here, and I hadn't found another place to hide it yet, so from now on I am always keeping the map with me. It's the safest place I could think of.

When the other girls in my room, start getting ready for bed, I try to talk to Isabelle again. I climb off my bed and walk over to the bunk beds directly in front of mine. I latch onto the ladder and join Isabelle in her bed, sitting directly in front of her. She isn't looking at me. I don't even think she realizes I'm here.

I turn her, so she is facing my direction and I grab both her hands.

"Isabelle, please snap out of it." I search her eyes, in the hope of finding a sliver of her old self, but nothing. She isn't looking at me but through me. Her hands are cold in mine, even after a warm shower.

"Come on Isabelle, I know you're in there. You have to fight whatever this is. I think I might have found a way out of here."

I'm hoping something that I say will wake her up, but I'm just reaching at this point. I trace my finger along the cut on her face, and she winces. Not because she came back to me but because she's in pain. Her body is telling her it hurts but her mind is keeping her from knowing what happened.

"We don't have to stay here, but I need you to remember. Think about the story you were telling me on the bus, about how your boyfriend cheated on you, but he was your soulmate. If you remember him, you'll be back to normal. Please, Isabelle, you do not deserve to be in here." There is no point in trying anymore but seeing her like this hurts. I've never met anyone who I connected with so quickly and knowing that the only reason she is in here is because of her dumb-ass boyfriend, is even worse.

This was my entire issue with the whole soulmate thing, people shouldn't be forced into these horrible relationships with creeps like him. How do people get so unlucky with who they have to end up with? And if they don't end up with them, they are forced here for the rest of their life? It's a sick joke. In what world is any of this fair? Somebody needs to put an end to this bullshit, but the only way to stop this is if I can get out of here and tell everyone that life in the Bunker isn't anything good. That the people who get sent down here are treated, with little to no respect, and have no choice in what happens to them.

Talking to Isabelle is a waste of time, so after trying to snap her out of it, I hop down from her bed. It's a little past ten, and it seems like everyone is falling asleep. I climb back into my bed and hope that I only have to stay here for one more day. If I'm lucky, I'll find the passage tomorrow, and I can get us out of here for good.

Chapter 25

Kayleigh

The next morning is the same routine. Everyone shoots awake at exactly 9:00 am, and by 9:30 am we are all standing by the door waiting to be escorted to breakfast. When we reach the eating quarters, we march directly to our table in the back corner. This time we had to wait a very long time to start eating. Once we were done, we all stood, leaving our plates on the table, just like yesterday.

Once again, we were the last group to leave. Walking through the halls, really stresses me out. I anticipated the abrupt

halt, so as to not cause a repeat of yesterday. When I woke up
this morning, I went over to check on Isabelle. The swelling of
her eye had gone down, but you could still see the marks the
guards left on her. We reached the workshop much quicker
than yesterday. The guards stayed in the room for the first thirty
minutes or so. I was sitting on the edge of my seat, waiting for
them to start bringing people out of the room. When they had
finally started taking people out, I sprang away from my desk
and continued searching the room from where I left off
yesterday.

I realized that I had more than half the room to search.
It felt like I had done more the day before but turns out I was
wrong. I tried being very meticulous, I wasn't going to risk
missing anything important.

Trying to find a secret passage in a room filled with
people, is not an easy task. I was crawling under tables and
squeezing by each person. I also needed to manage my own
station without setting off any alarm. A blaring noise would
come out of my station if I don't hit my button within each time
frame. It happened once, and it freaked me out so bad, that the
next time the guard left the room, I stayed at my table and
didn't move a muscle.

Eventually, when I grew the courage to continue, I was
quicker. I had gotten through a good chunk of the room before

the guards escorted me out. I tried speeding through the process so I could get back to looking, but the guard slowed me down. Everything is so perfectly timed here, which is a blessing and a curse.

There were only a handful of people left who needed to be escorted out, and I only had a few more stations to search. I still hadn't found anything, and I was growing more and more agitated the longer I looked.

I tried to stay positive because I managed to have only two more stations to look through, with two more people still left to be taken out. It was Spencer's station and a girl from my room. I quickly search her workspace and was about to look through Spencer's when the door sprang open. I freeze. A wave of panic coursed through my body. This guard, who couldn't be more than 5' 6" walks into the room. I take a quick scan of the room, starting on the side that I am standing on. I managed to sneak behind Spencer, so they do not see me very well. My biggest worry was when he would finally take note of my empty station. He noticed someone was missing and rushed out the door. My heart sank to my stomach and sprinted to the other side of the room. Dodging people as I make my way through the workshop, I am completely out of breath by the time the door swings back open.

Another guard walks in accompanying the short guy who was here before. When the small guy points towards my station, the big guard speaks up.

"You stupid or something?"

"I promise you; no one was there before."

"Oh yeah? So, you think she just magically fell from the sky?"

"Fuck off buddy. I know what I saw."

"I'm sure you did." The bigger guy taps him on the shoulder and walks back out the door.

I keep waiting for the little guy to walk out behind him, but he stayed by the door. For the remainder of the time that we were working, he was watching me like a hawk. I hadn't finished searching the place, I only had one more section to look through. The realization hits me that the secret passage that I have been looking for must be in the same station that Spencer is working at.

When time was up, we were escorted back to our rooms. The door shut behind us, and all the girls took the opportunity to clean off and put on a fresh pair of clothes. I look towards the clock and realize that it's still early, so I wait a while until everyone starts getting ready for bed.

I scan over the map a few more times, trying to see where I would find Spencer's room, but nothing on the map tells me where he could be staying. After a while, I conclude that I'm going to have to sneak around the hallways to find him because there is no chance, I am leaving him in here. I just need to act quickly.

The girls eventually all make their way into their beds, which is when I put on the jeans and a shirt I found on my chest. I walk over to Isabelle staring into her soulless eyes, I tell her that I will find a way out of here and that I will come back for her.

I hop off the ladder leading up to her bed and walk towards the door. I make sure I still have the map in my pocket and take one more look around the room, I hope to never see it again.

When the door opens, I feel this gust of wind hit my face, and I start running down the halls, looking for Spencer.

Chapter 26

Kayleigh

I quickly make my way down the halls looking for Spencer's room. Considering I have zero clue where his room could be, it takes me a lot longer than I was hoping for. I walked into several bunks, all the same style, all with people my age sleeping.

I turn down a few more corners until I finally see the room I was looking for. I can see Spencer sleeping in his bunk bed through the small window on the door. This huge feeling of relief washed over me, but before I could make my way through the door, I heard these footsteps coming from behind me. I quickly step my way towards the adjacent wall.

I press myself against it and hope that whoever is making their way down the hallway, doesn't turn down here and see me, or I'm for sure going to be caught.

Their steps get louder, and I can see their feet getting closer and closer to where I'm standing. I am holding my breath. It looks like they are about to turn right into me but instead, they walk toward and push open the door I was just looking through.

Two guards had just walked through the door to get into Spencer's room. One of them is tall and the other one is short. They look like the two guards from the workshop. I can't help but stare at the size of the guns both guys have attached to their hips.

A few minutes pass and they come out of the room. My heart drops to the floor as I see that they have Spencer squished between the two of them, holding onto him by his wrists. He isn't being dragged but they are moving faster than his feet can move.

"Shit." I say under my breath. The small guard looks back and I throw my hands over my mouth. Luckily, he doesn't see me and turns back around, I try trailing behind them.

I leave some space between us but still try to follow them as closely as possible. I'm near enough that I can hear the two of them speaking.

"Turns out one of the subjects isn't under Storm's control anymore. She is freaking out."

"Really? So does that mean I was right before?"

"Huh?"

"With the missing worker from this afternoon. I was right."

"Can't believe I'm going to admit it, but chances are yes, you were right. But don't let that shit get to your head. You're still useless."

"That's the closest thing to a compliment you've ever said to me."

"Shut up."

"So, does she have an idea of who it could be?"

"All she knows is that it's one of the new ones. So, she's going one by one dosing them with more serum."

"Won't that mess with them though? I thought I heard the doctor say people couldn't withstand a double dose."

The big one looks down, "Like I give a shit, I would rather be on this side of it anyways. Remember how it felt when we were under their control? I'm just glad she decided to make us guards." The small guy nods in agreement.

"But why did we have to come grab this guy in the middle of the night? My shift had just ended when you came knocking."

"Not sure, I was just told to come get his ass, and you pissed me off earlier, so I grabbed you also."

"Seriously dude. Not cool." The bigger guy chuckles in return.

They reach this narrow passageway but don't walk down it. Instead, a piercing alarm goes off, followed by a message.

Code Red. I repeat there is a Code Red. Will all available personnel make their way to the base for further instruction...

The message plays on a loop.

"Code red?"

"Means someone is missing. I guess they figured out who isn't under their control anymore. I overheard Seth and Wells being told to grab someone from the girl's room, I'm pretty sure it's that girl that Storm has been obsessed with, maybe it's her."

They leave Spencer in front of the passageway and run in the opposite direction. I'm guessing Code Red takes precedence, but I'm shocked they just left him there.

I don't react right away until it finally clicks in my head. I hear the alarm a few more times before I realize they know they are looking for me.

"Damn it," I yell a little too loud.

I spring forward from the shadows and grab Spencer by his arms. I'm dragging him back to where I was hiding. It's not easy bringing him back, it feels like he is resisting me, but I use all my strength to get him there quickly. I grab a hold of his face and look into his eyes. I almost don't recognize the man I'm holding in my hands. I pull him towards my face and kiss him regardless.

It only took me a few seconds to snap out of the trance, so I expect almost an immediate response, but when he doesn't come to, I pull myself away from him. I feel tears running down my face because I hoped that would've worked. I try again, and again, but nothing changes.

His face is still stoned cold, showing zero emotion. *Did I wait too long?* Every possible scenario starts running through my head. *Do I need to leave him here? If I get out, would I be able to come back and save him? No! You can't do that.* Everything in me tells me to save myself and leave him for now, but when I look at him, I know there was a reason we were down here together. I can't escape without his help. So no, I cannot leave him. I will never leave him. I have to wake him up, but I just don't know how.

I hear footsteps running down the adjacent hallway, and panic starts to climb in me. I pull him deeper down the hallway we are hiding in, trying to avoid the noise because if we are to be caught there is no telling what would happen. I pull him down to the floor, and we are sitting facing each other now in the darkness of the hall. I take his hand and wipe the lone tear that's falling from my eye.

"I know you don't remember anything, and I know we said we will get through this together, but I can't risk us both being stuck here. If they catch us, we will never get out of this place. I think I found a way out. I've been studying the map and the passage to get out of here is in your workspace. Spencer if you are hearing any of the things I'm telling you, please know that if I do manage to get out of here, I will come back for you."
What are you saying, you can't leave Spencer here.

My mouth is moving, and I hear the words coming out of it, but why am I telling him all of this? I don't want to leave him. I can't. I love him.

I love him.

"You have changed my life in more ways than one. You gave me hope for something bigger and having to leave you here shatters my heart. I can't imagine going back to society without you next to me. I need you," I swipe my fingers over his lips and across his jaw. I push his hair that has fallen in front of his eyes, they were the first things I noticed about him when I first saw him, "Spencer," my voice is shaky but I'm trying not to cry again, "I love you, forever and always." I begin to get up from the corner of the hallway when I feel his hand grip mine. I turn around to see those beautiful green eyes gleaming into mine, a smirk crosses his face.

"You love me?"

Before I could answer him, another announcement plays over the speakers.

ATTENTION: All personnel please be advised that the Code Red has turned into Code Black. I repeat we are now in a Code Black. The missing person in question is Kayleigh Harris, and there is a chance she is armed. *

Oh shit.

We need to go.

Fast.

Chapter 27
SPENCER

She loves me.

I can't believe she loves me.

She grabs my hand and starts pulling me down the hallway. I try slowing her down, but she is persistent. There is this announcement that keeps playing over the speakers that has gotten her worried.

"Kayleigh, can we just stop for two seconds, so you can explain to me what is going on."

She is struggling to regain her breath. We stop. I give her a few seconds to compose herself.

"You know the map that Kate gave me?" I nod, I hope I know where this is going, "well, I found the passage that Mason Clark used."

"Kayleigh that's amazing." I lift her up and spin her around. "Where is it?"

"Funny thing." Her eyes are wandering, avoiding me at all costs, "I'm kind of hoping it's where your workstation was."

"What do you mean, kind of hoping? This is all a hunch?" My voice grows a bit louder after every word.

"Well, I never got the chance to look there when we were working this morning, because I didn't want to risk you coming out of the trance. And I almost got caught by the guards. But the good thing is, it's the only spot in that room that I haven't checked."

"This morning?"

She nods her head, does this mean I went the entire day, under the control of the Bunker? I remember vaguely going to see the doctor early in the morning, but everything blurs together at one point.

"How long have I been under this trance Kayleigh?"

"Over 24 hours."

"OVER 24 HOURS?"

She nods her head.

It hadn't felt like I was in a trance for too long, but knowing it's been more than a day makes me feel terrible. My mind keeps flashing back to the doctors, in hopes of remembering some of the conversations that I had. But after I closed my eyes, the next thing I remembered was hearing Kayleigh's voice.

"So, you're telling me, we don't actually know if the passage is there?" She gives me a sheepish smile. "Well, guess we better start moving." I reach for her hands and when our palms touch, I feel a shiver down my spine. Even though we are nowhere near normal, having her with me makes everything feel all right.

"Lead the way, Satan." She smacks my shoulder with her free hand, and I can't help but smile. I hate to say it, but this girl is getting stronger because that smack is definitely going to leave a mark. She then starts pulling me down the halls.

She is flying down these hallways, taking each turn quickly but carefully. I don't know how she's doing it because everything just looks the same. In no time at all we are both stopped in front of a steel door. I assume it's the workroom, so I immediately lunge for the door trying to get it open. I crash into the door, it doesn't budge.

"It's locked."

Kayleigh walks up beside me and tries for herself, when she has no luck she slams her hand against the door, "Shit."

Just to the left of the door, there is a spot to swipe a keycard. I point it out to her, "We need to find the key."

Kayleigh immediately runs down one of the adjacent hallways, when she gets to the end, she motions for me to join her.

"Listen."

"What am I listening to exactly?"

"The code that they called is still only for me, so they don't know yet that you are out of the trance."

"So?"

"Do I have to figure everything out myself? We can use you as a decoy. You stand in the hallway, and we wait until a guard comes towards you. Hopefully, it's only one, so we can jump him."

"Should I be concerned that you seem really excited to jump someone?"

"Maybe." She nudges me into the open hallway. "Go stand there."

I trust Kayleigh one hundred percent, so if she tells me to go stand in the middle of the hallway to be the decoy, I will.

Luckily for us, it does not take long for a lone guard to come stumbling down the corridor.

"Hey, you shouldn't be out here." This guard must be dense, if I actually was in a trance, how would I be able to respond to him?

"Oh right. You things can't speak." He is a serious pain in my ass. Just as he is about to grab a hold of me, Kayleigh jumps onto his back. I'm in awe of what she just did that I am frozen in place, but the deep cut of Kayleigh's voice brings me back down to earth.

"You going to help me out, Jackass?"

"Right, sorry." I spring towards them and help my girl tie the guard up. It takes the two of us a few seconds to get the guard under control. I wish I could take credit for tying him up, but Kayleigh did most of the work. I kind of just stood there and looked pretty. I would like to think my presence was enough but who am I kidding, I was useless.

"Thank god you are easy to look at, because holy hell, Jackass, you are useless sometimes."

"I'd like to take that as a compliment, but damn Satan, I didn't know you were this feisty."

"There's a lot you still don't know about me, Jackass." She winks toward me, and I can feel a flutter in my stomach,

"Now grab the key card and be productive, we need to get out of here fast."

I search the guard and find the card tucked away in one of his pockets. We leave him in the corner of a hallway, so he is out of sight. Just as we were about to walk off towards the door, we decided to put something in his mouth so he couldn't scream for help. *That is something I can take credit for.* When that's finished up, and we know the guard will no longer be an issue, the two of us make our way back to the workshop as fast as we possibly can.

"I really hope this works." I swipe the keycard, but the lights flash red, I try again but no change. "Fuck. It's not working."

"Let me see." I hand her the card, "Spencer." I look at her as she reaches out for my arm, "It was the wrong way, Sweetie." She is practically hollering with laughter.

"Shut up." I push the door open once she gets the keycard to work and walk into the room.

I realize I have no recollection of ever being in here, so I let Kayleigh take charge and have her tell me what to do.

She brings us to the back corner of the room and starts pushing things around. I'm standing in awe of her while she rummages around the workspace, "What do you think we are even looking for?"

"I'm assuming some sort of door, so just look for that."

We look around a little while longer, I'm scanning the back wall, the floor, and the ceiling, hoping to find a hidden door. I'm looking all over, but everything seems to be normal, so just as I am about to move on to another section, I glance towards a random curtain hanging from the wall. I never thought much of it, but that would be a perfect place to hide a secret door. It must have seemed too obvious at first because I was so close to leaving it unchecked. When I reach for the curtain and pull it back slightly, I am shocked and quite relieved by my discovery.

"Kayleigh," I call out, "I think I found something."

She comes running around the table to help me push the curtain out of the way completely. A small door appears where the curtain once was. We lock eyes with each other and push it open revealing a small ladder heading downwards.

The two of us are hesitant at first, thinking that maybe this could be a trap. But time is not on our side.

"You feel good about this Kayleigh?"

"No, but what choice do we have, right?" Just as we are about to head down the ladder, we hear rattling at the main door.

"Somebody get me a keycard, now!"

"They have to be in there, someone's card was used right here 10 minutes ago."

"For Christ's sake, somebody knock down this door." That last voice was Regina Storm. When I hear her speaking, parts of my memory come back to early this morning when she was asking me to be one of her guards.

I turn towards Kayleigh, "We got to move fast." I send her down first, making sure she gets out of this room, in case they get in before we get down.

When she starts climbing down the ladder, I try my best to move everything back into its place, so they have trouble finding the door. Just as I get far enough down the ladder for the door to close, I hear a trample of people storming the room.

Chapter 28

SPENCER

I race down the ladder as fast as I possibly can, but my hands are sweating, and I lose my grip several times.

"Hurry Spencer." Hearing the desperation in her voice makes me move even faster. I miss the last few bearings and fall to the ground. "Oh my god," Kayleigh bends down to help me up, "Are you alright?" I jump back up and shake off any dirt that got on me.

"Yeah, I'm fine, but we have to go now. They're right on our heels." Without a moment's notice, we both start running down these new hallways.

I look around the halls we are passing by and find major similarities to the halls that we were just running through. I realized that I shouldn't have wasted my time putting everything back in place because the people running this place must know this passage is here. The lights are flashing red, and the alarm is still blaring. The halls are much narrower; the two of us can barely fit standing next to each other, I let Kayleigh lead us, so she can set the pace.

"What does the map say once we get to this point?"

"Nothing."

"What do you mean nothing? What are we supposed to do from here?"

"Run."

"Great. We have no idea where this could possibly take us."

"Hey, Jackass?"

"Yes, Satan?"

"I know you may have some strong emotions right now, but for the love of god please shut up and run."

"Whatever you say." I am biting my tongue because not having a plan right now is freaking me out. I still trust Kayleigh, and I think that we can figure this out ourselves, but don't get me wrong, not knowing what happens at the end of these passages, scares the shit out of me. I do what she tells me though, and I keep running for my life.

We have been running for what feels like forever, turning down hallway after hallway, not knowing how close they are behind us and not knowing where we are going to end up. We made several turns down different corridors before we reach a fork in the road. Two separate ways to go. Kayleigh and I look at each other, but neither one of us has a clue which way we should go.

"Shit. Which way do we go?"

"I don't know Spence; the map doesn't tell us anything else." She's pacing in front of me with her hands on her forehead.

"Well, we need to decide quickly. Who knows how close they are."

We are spending way too much time trying to decide which way to go. Just as I am about to drag her down the hall, we hear it. The loud noise of boots marching behind us in unison.

"I wouldn't do that if I were you." We both turn around to see maybe half a dozen guards standing at the end of the hallway. "We got this whole place secured. There's no getting out of here." I'm trying to size these guys up, calculating my chances of being able to take on all six of them. My chances aren't looking great. I've been in a few fights at school, but never against this many people and never by myself. The guard who is doing the talking leans over to the much smaller guy next to him and whispers something into his ear. He walks off behind the rest of them while saying something into his walkie-talkie.

"Stay where you are and put your hands up in the air."

"And what if we don't," Kayleigh is grabbing onto my hand from behind me, I subconsciously moved in front of her to keep her at a greater distance from the guards. Kayleigh is whispering something in my ear but it's hard for me to hear, the alarm is too loud and the grunts coming from the other end of the hallway are not helping.

I squeeze her hand to let her know everything is going to be okay, just as Regina Storms pushes through the row of guards. The sheer sight of her brings back my memory from this morning.

"You kids are hard to track down. You did some nice work for one of my guards up there. If you weren't such a flight risk, I would offer you both a chance to work as guards. But since Spencer already turned me down once, I don't find it necessary to waste my breath."

"What is she talking about Spencer?"

"You didn't tell her, that I offered you the ultimate protection? That I was going to put you up in a nice room, for your simple cooperation? Disappointing Spencer. I expected more from you."

"Just let us go." Kayleigh has emerged from behind my back but is still holding a tight grip on my hand. "We did what you guys wanted! We found our soulmate. Why can't we just leave?"

"Oh, you poor thing. Did you honestly believe that if you were to find your soulmate down here after seeing everything that you did and causing this amount of panic, we would let you go?" She patiently waits for a response, but when she doesn't receive one, she continues. "We can't have you two telling the world what we do down here. We would be shut down in a second."

"We swear we won't say a thing. Just let us go. We don't even know what it is you guys are doing down here. All I've seen is that you put us to work."

It's not until Kayleigh says this, do I question where the rest of the people are. The workspace had only thirty or so stations, so where were the rest of the kids from the same day as we were? Where is everyone else from every other year?

"Well, if you swear, I guess that's all right."

I let go of Kayleigh's hand, "Really?"

"No," she laughs, "you must seriously be dense."

"Hey! Don't you dare talk about him like that you grotesque bitch."

"Sweetie, grow up. You had plenty of time to find each other before the deadline, but instead, you were both tricked by some wannabe cheerleader."

"What do you mean tricked by some cheerleader?" Kayleigh asks.

"How do you know Josie?" When the question leaves my mouth, a small grin appears on Regina's face.

"I'm sure the two of you have had thoughts about me looking familiar. Right?"

We surprisingly nod in unison. "Have either of you figured it out yet?" She waits patiently for one of us to answer, but I still struggle to place her. Kayleigh makes the realization, after a few seconds.

"No…"

"Guess someone figured it out. Care to share with the rest of the class?"

"Everyone thinks you died."

"Daddy didn't want anyone knowing that I run this place, so he came up with the idea of making everyone think I died in that car crash."

"Can somebody please explain to me what is going on?"

"Regina Storm is actually Regina Carson."

My mouth opens in disbelief, "Carson? As in my psycho ex-girlfriend, Carson?"

"Don't you ever talk about my sister that way? Only I can call her a psycho, you have no right."

"Sister? You're the sister Josie always talked about?"

"That would be me. Now that we are all up to speed, can we please call it a day, and you two can stop making such a spectacle? My job is usually easier than this with all the other inmates."

"Come on Regina, you've known me my whole life, your sister and I used to be friends, I don't even know why she started hating me so much. Why can't you just let us go."

"Josie only started hating you, because you had more friends than she did."

"She was the most popular girl in school, how did I have more friends than her?"

"Josie is special, it may have looked like she had a lot of friends, but her seeing you get really close with Sadie and Kate, pushed her over the edge. When you started to hang out with them more than her, she vowed to ruin your life."

"Are you fucking serious? She decided to ruin my life because she was insecure about who I was friends with?"

"What can I say, my sister has a mind of her own, but she is daddy's little princess, so anything she says goes."

"Come on, let us go, Regina."

"Please, we have been waiting for the two of you for years now, it's the most excited I've ever been. You think Josie is psycho, who do you think she learnt it from? Josie came to talk to me when our father was here for his 'annual' drop-in. Told me there was this girl she never wanted to see again, I assumed it was you because I never liked you either, so I left the soulmate list open on my computer and she found your name. She's the one who takes over here once I can't anymore. Couldn't risk making her angry. She always did get her way when I was at home. Anyways it's more fun watching people freak out over these things like both of you did. After a while, this gets kind of boring, waiting for the two of you kept my spirits alive."

I hear Kayleigh whispering the word bitch. I can't tell which Carson sister she is referring to, but both would work perfectly fine right about now.

"What do you guys do when the next deadline comes around?" I try to stop myself from asking, but it just spills out, "This can't be everyone. What do you do with the other people?" I'm practically screaming now waiting for an answer, but seeing a small smirk cross her face tells me everything that I need to know.

"That's what you don't want us knowing, isn't it? What do you do? Kill them? Ship them somewhere else? What is it, Regina?" My voice is cracking in between every word. How can our society be okay with what these people are doing? Innocent people are being 'taken care of' because they couldn't find a soulmate? That is absolute insanity. And to think that the girl I once believed cared for me, and who was once Kayleigh's greatest friend, had no issue in sending us down here, knowing full well what happens, makes me sick.

"Let's not make this any harder than it needs to be. Just come with us." Storm is walking a bit ahead of the guards now, getting closer to the two of us. A part of me doesn't want to keep running, but the other part is screaming at me to get Kayleigh out of here. I see on her face that she is still reflecting on what Regina just said. I make the decision for both of us. I grab a hold of her hand and start sprinting down the corridor to the right of us. Leaving Regina Storm and the guards in our wake.

They are close behind us, but we have gotten enough separation for now, we refuse to let up. We just run until we can't anymore. I'm using all the built-up emotions to keep us moving forward, if I take a second to process what truly is going on down here, I may crumble.

I can't do that to Kayleigh.

Not now.

Not ever.

We have to keep pushing.

We have been running for what feels like forever, it's hard to tell, where we even are, with every turn we take, the halls look more and more alike.

"Spencer," I'm struggling to catch my breath, "can we please take a second? I've never run this much in my life."

He reluctantly stops, realizing how much I was straining to keep up with him. "Sure, we can stop for a few seconds."

I hunch over placing my hands on my knees, "How are you not out of breath."

"Years of Coach making us run laps around the field." He walks over behind me and rubs the bottom of my back. "Not everyone can be as athletic as me."

I stand up and playfully push him backwards. He tries hiding the grin that appears on his face but there's no use. He grabs my hips and pulls me close to him. "You said something to me earlier, that we never had a chance to talk about."

"Oh yeah?" I'm peering up into his eyes, "And what did I say?" I know exactly what he is referring to, but I won't make it easy for him.

He leans in and kisses me, starting at my lips and working his way down to my neck. I want this moment to last forever, but I know right now is not the place. I tap his shoulder and he meets my eyes once again. He hugs me tightly and kisses the side of my forehead. "I love you too."

I peer up to look him in his eyes, "Spencer?"

He looks down at me, to show that he is listening.

"Did you consider working with Storm, as one of her guards?"

"Do you want me to be honest with you?"

"Ideally, yes."

"Well, for a brief moment I did consider it, thinking that I would be able to look after you, but I slipped up, and they figured out that I might have seen you, so Regina took all chances away."

I push myself off him. "You slipped up? Is that why we are being chased right now? Cause you mentioned me?"

He has a worried look on his face, "I never meant for all of this to happen."

Spencer sounds genuine, but I can't shake the feeling that everything that's happening right now, is because he slipped up. I thought he was smarter than that. I face the opposite way and shake my head. I feel him walk up behind me and wrap his arms around my waist. "Kayleigh, I'm sorry. I never wanted to put you in danger, I wasn't thinking."

I twist around to face him again, "I believe you, and I love you."

"I love you too."

I never knew that four words can affect someone so much, but I can't dwell on it for too long, who knows how close Regina and her minions are? I grab Spencer's hand and we begin running through the hall yet again.

We keep running and running until we can't anymore. I can feel my chest closing with every step I take. My breath is ragged, but I know we can't risk stopping for another pause. Spencer has slowed down countless times for me, but I refuse to be the reason we get caught. I dig down deep to find any stored energy and run as if my life depended on it, because right now it does.

I let Spencer run a little ahead of me, allowing him to see if we are going the proper way. A little up ahead I see him stop and throw his hands up in the air. As I approach him, I call out, "What's the matter?"

"It's a dead end."

"Shit, seriously." I see him nodding his head. I run up beside him, as if something will change if I was there. I smack the wall with my fists, we must have gone the wrong way, but we can't turn back now. When I turn back around to face the hallway we just ran down, just out of view I see something hidden on the wall. There's a ladder that leads toward a manhole.

It's our way out.

"Spencer." I tap him on the shoulder.

"What?"

"Look." He follows my gaze and sees the ladder. "We did it, we actually found the way out of here."

"No, Kayleigh, you did it."

The only emotion I feel right now is relief, I jump into Spencer's arms celebrating the idea that we are the only other people besides Mason Clark, to have found the way out of this place.

"You go up first, I'll be right behind you."

"You promise?"

He grabs my hand and kisses it, "Right behind you."

I take my first few steps up the ladder when I hear her voice for another time.

"Get off the ladder, Kayleigh. I already told the both of you we can't have you getting out of here."

We were so close.

Spencer turns back towards me, his voice no louder than a whisper, "Go, keep climbing." My entire body freezes in place, I can't move despite his pleas. By the looks of it, we would have enough time for the both of us to get out of here before they could even get close to us.

"Do not make me ask again. Get off the ladder, and we won't have to do this the hard way."

"Kayleigh please keep going." So many things are going through my head right now, but if I keep going who knows if Spencer will follow me? I can't risk him being stuck down here himself. The first time I saw him down here, I told myself we would be in this together, with everything we've been through I am not going back on what I said.

I take a step down from the ladder and grab Spencer's arm. His head falls between his shoulders. I know what he's thinking but leaving him was never going to be an option.

"Smart girl."

Spencer moves in front of me, blocking me from Storm and the guard's view. "You better stay back, Storm."

"Or what?"

"Only one of us needs to get out of here, to expose what's truly going on." I squeeze his arm to let him know, he can continue, "I can assure you; I can slow you down just enough for Kayleigh to get free. It only takes one."

It's a good thing I'm standing behind him, this way he won't be able to see the trickle of tears falling down my face.

"Spencer, I'm not going to leave you." Only he can hear me.

"How sweet are you? Did you ever treat my sister like this? You playing the hero?" Her voice is condescending, she acts exactly like Josie, with no care in the world for anyone but themselves.

I try not to focus on what she is saying, the only person that has my attention is the guy standing right in front of me. His whole body is tense, veins popping out of his arms, sweat dripping off the side of his head, and he is trembling from head to toe. But his demeanor towards Regina has not changed once. He is still standing tall, shoulders out, making him look bigger than he really is. Spencer is in full protection mode over me right now, and I don't know if I should kiss him, or tell him he doesn't need to do this alone.

"I'm losing my patience over here, Brown. The two of you better stay where you are, or I swear we will do this the hard way."

"Just let us leave you bitch." His tone is harsh, and straight to the point. You can hear the fatigue in his voice though, he told me that he was woken up early in the morning, and barely slept. He is running on only a few hours of sleep.

Neither one of us want the situation to escalate, but Regina is not standing down.

"Don't test me, tough guy." She draws her gun from her belt buckle and points it directly at us. I gasp at the sight of it. "I told you I'm losing my patience, and I wasn't making any jokes. If you both want to survive this, you better start listening."

Spencer's hands shoot up in the air, posing no threat to Regina or the guards. "Hold up, there's no need for this to escalate Regina. We can talk this out."

She isn't backing down. I can feel the room getting smaller and smaller as I stare down at the barrel of the gun. I've never been on this side of a gun before, and my palms start to sweat.

She tries taking a step forward but we both yell out. "Regina, stop." our voices are stern and in unison, "how 'bout we make a deal? You willing to hear us out?"

She stops in her tracks but still has a tight grip on her gun.

"We can stop this right now."

"Spencer, what are you talking about?" He brushes me off and continues speaking to Regina.

"You let Kayleigh go, and I will willingly come with you."

"Spencer, no! I am not leaving you here."

"Come on Regina, you don't need the both of us, I will do whatever you need me to do. Work as your personal slave, work as a guard, anything you need I'll be your go-to guy." I'm a wreck, tears are pouring down my face, I cannot believe the words coming out of his mouth.

Silence fills the tunnels.

No one wants to be the first to speak. I can see Regina processing the offer in her mind, the gears in her head are spinning, and so are mine.

"Kayleigh, look at me." He is wiping the tears from my face. "Everything is going to be all right. I need you to trust me."

"Please Spencer," my voice breaks, "I can't leave you down here. We can figure this out together. We can stay here together if that's what you want."

"Kayleigh, I promise, it's going to be all right," he grabs the side of my face with his hand, and I lean into it. When I say go, you're going to climb up the ladder as fast as you can."

I'm shaking my head in protest, "No Spencer, I don't know what I would do without you."

"Kayleigh, look at me." He grabs my chin and moves my face so I am looking directly at him, and barely over a whisper Spencer tells me again, "When I say go, you climb as fast as you can."

In a much louder voice, Spencer keeps talking as if we are having an entirely different conversation.

"I will always be with you; I couldn't live with myself if something were to happen to you. Everything that we dealt with this year, has been worth every good thing. Life was never worth living until I met you. Every morning I would wake up excited to see you, excited for all the ways you would rip into me during class. You made me feel, for the first time in a long time, Kayleigh." I feel like the only person in the world right now, "You are the first person I have truly allowed myself to open up to, I feel safe when I am with you." He is backing me up towards the ladder, and all I can manage to do is nod.

A slight grin appears on his face, and he winks at me, "I love you."

I lunge forward and kiss him, "I love you too." I forget for a second where we are because when Spencer talks to me the world around us disappears, he makes all the bad things feel good, and all the good things feel amazing. When the moment is up, I look into Spencer's eyes one more time, and he mouths the words, "Now..."

I spring into action and climb the ladder two steps at a time. It's not until I feel the whole thing shake, do I notice that Spencer is just below me following me directly at my heels. In one single moment, all my senses defy me. I can no longer hear the commotion coming from beneath us, and everything is moving in slow motion. I see Spencer, motioning for me to keep going, but I'm frozen in place. I'm stuck on this ladder not knowing what to do, but the moment I hear a piercing noise, I break the silence I created.

Chapter 29

Kayleigh

"Oh shit."

"Keep going, Kayleigh." His voice sounds almost breathless, but he still manages to speak, "Don't stop now. We're almost there."

I'm struggling to keep going, hearing the gunshots behind me, is making me flinch every time someone pulls the trigger. I see parts of the wall coming off, as the bullets make contact, and thank my lucky stars that nothing had hit me. *Knock on wood, but they sure do suck at using those guns.*

I manage to get up to the manhole and push the lid open, I climb out the top and reach my hand in to help pull Spencer out of there. He winces as I pull, but once we both have our feet on the ground, we slam the lid shut.

"We did it." I'm twirling in circles, taking in the fresh air that surrounds us. "Spencer, I can't believe we did it."

"Yeah." His voice remains breathless, and I jerk around to face him. He is hunched over grabbing onto his side.

"Spencer?" Before I could finish saying his name, he collapses. I manage to break most of his fall and gently bring us both to the ground.

I move his hand to the side to reveal a deep burgundy red staining his abdomen area.

"No." My voice is hushed but in pain, I thought we were done. We made it out. *How could this still be going on?*

He was shot.

I'm running my hands through his hair, "I got you, you're gonna be okay." I don't know how I manage to form words, but they come out smoothly. I do everything in my power to keep him from freaking out.

"Kayleigh," he looks down at his stomach, "it hurts."

"I know, Baby, but just focus on me. You're going to be all right."

I couldn't tell if his hands were shaking or mine, so I linked our hands together to prevent them from moving.

"Spencer, just look at me, you have to keep your eyes open, okay? I'm right here. I'm not going anywhere."

"Kayleigh, listen to me, I'm going to be alright, go find someone, I'll be right here when you get back."

"Spence, I'm not going to leave you. Nothing you can say will make me leave you right now."

"I know," he says softly, "I know." His voice is breathless.

I kiss the top of his forehead, *why did he get shot? How could she shoot him? We never should have gone up the ladder.*

"Kayls look at me," I look at him, tears flowing down my face, "I promise you everything will be okay." How can he say something like this right now, obviously everything isn't going to be all right. "Remember what you told me about what you thought a soulmate should be?" I shake my head. "You said that a soulmate should be someone who is willing to sacrifice themselves for the person they love." I know I'm losing him; his eyes are struggling to stay open now. "I'm glad I was able to be the person to stand in front of a bullet for you."

"Spencer, you got to keep your eyes open. Please just hold on." There is no stopping the tears now; I am a mess and

I feel every emotion rising in my body. "Just keep your eyes open, and I'll go find someone to help."

With all his efforts, he manages to nod his head ever so slightly.

"Oh Kayleigh," he tries his hardest to reach for my face, but struggles, "I will love you forever and always."

"Please, Spencer." My whole-body trembles as I hold onto him, my grip is tight, I do not want to let him go. I think to myself, if I let go of him, he will be gone. I can't lose him, I just got him back; I promised I would do whatever it took to save him. "Please stay awake, don't give up on me now." I wrap him up into a hug and feel his last attempt at a breath.

And it was that moment, he was gone. I look down to see his eyes piercing up at me, there is no life in them anymore, so I gently close his eyelids, and kiss the top of his forehead.

"I love you too." I feel a tear trickle down the side of my face.

All it took was one moment.

One moment to lose the one person I never knew I needed.

I felt a part of me disappearing.

My whole world had just collapsed…

Chapter 30

Kayleigh

All I feel is numb. My body, my mind, my everything is numb.

The boy I loved, was lifeless in front of me. Blood all over my hands and pooled on the floor. His blood.

I look up towards the sky, and the moon and stars light up the night. But the atmosphere around me is somber. Although the night is clear, everything feels dark. This daze washes over me, as I stare at the lifeless boy in front of me. I want to scream and I want to cry, but all I can picture is that sickening grin forming on Regina's face, knowing that one bullet managed to pierce one of us. All I want to do is go back down there and charge her. Make her feel a sliver of the pain I am feeling right about now. I want her to experience the pain Spencer had just felt.

But despite how good beating Regina's ass would feel, that's not what Spencer would have wanted. He stood in front of a bullet because he wanted me to get out of the Bunker, because he remembered that I once said that a real soulmate would sacrifice themselves for another person. Spencer was the only one to understand me, he did what I had unknowingly asked him to do. He sacrificed himself so I could save myself. Spencer is my hero, and my forever, I cannot let him die in vain.

I stand up despite not wanting to leave him. But I'm not strong enough to carry him through the woods. I look down at my hands and decide to wipe the blood on my jeans.

I hear yells coming from beneath me, Regina and the guards must be trying to climb the ladder. I can't be caught out here, so I look down at Spencer for one last time, "I love you forever and always."

I turn towards the open land surrounding us and begin to run.

The adrenaline kicks in, so I run and run until I physically can't anymore.

...

After running for what feels like an eternity, I reach a forest. I swerve between the trees, trying to find a way out of there. I don't know how close anyone is behind me, or if anyone even followed me. When I feel somewhat safe, I lean up against a tree, trying to catch my breath.

I see flashlights moving toward me from the corner of my eye. When I turn to keep running, this sharp pain travels through my leg. I look down to see patches of blood pooling from my calf. One of the bullets must've hit me also, but with everything that happened the adrenaline prevented me from feeling it, until now.

I rip part of my t-shirt and tie a knot just above the wound. It hurts like hell, but the bleeding slows until it completely stops. I try pushing through the pain, but I cannot move fast, I'm limping through the forest as quickly as I can, but the flashlights are getting closer and closer.

The only thought running through my mind, is that if I get caught out here, Spencer died for nothing. No amount of pain will stop me from making sure that the boy I love did not die for nothing. I tell myself that the end of the forest couldn't be too far, but the more time I spend in here, the darker it becomes, and I am starting to lose my way. I push myself to my limits and refuse to give up.

The forest goes on forever. I have no clue where I am, and all the trees are beginning to merge. Everywhere I look I see the same dense forest, nothing but trees that engulf the land. I hear cars in the distance, so I must be near a road. I listen for more noise and allow myself to follow it. I limp through the trees until I finally find a street.

I pray to myself that a car will somehow stop, but I have no idea what time it is. For all I know it could be the middle of the night. One or two cars, pass by but show no sign of slowing down. I use all my excess energy in trying to flag them down, by the time they pass, I can barely stand up on my own two feet.

"Kayleigh." I hear a low voice calling my name, repeatedly.

I turn back around to see if the lights are still following me, and they are. They have gotten closer and closer; I can practically reach out my arm and touch them. I don't have enough in me anymore to keep running. *This is it? Spencer died for nothing.*

The pain in my leg is excruciating now. I can barely stand up, I must've lost a lot of blood because my vision is starting to give, and everything is going blurry. I try to hold on a little while longer, but I'm not sure how much more time I have left in me.

I try running forward, but my leg stays on the ground. It won't move anymore, and the flashlights are close. I pray that they aren't guards from the Bunker because I can't keep running. I hope for a miracle, but mentally try to prepare for the worst.

I feel a hand reach out for my arm, and I reluctantly turn back towards the person, knowing that I didn't put up enough of a fight.

But when I see who it is, and who is touching me, I let myself collapse. They wrap their arms around me, and I finally let myself go, I let myself be vulnerable again.

"Kayleigh." They seemed surprised, but a small sense of relief filled their voice.

My voice is shaky, and I can barely stand on my leg. I somehow manage to get out the name of the person standing right in front of me, "Alec". A sense of relief overpowers me, and I finally let myself go. My eyes fully close knowing that I got away but left Spencer behind.

EPILOGUE

Kayleigh
A week later

"Spencer no!" My eyes burst open, and I am covered in sweat. My heart is racing, as I relive the moment of Spencer taking his final breath. I wipe away the few tears that trickle down my cheek. I look around the room. I see that I am sitting in Alec's bed. I vaguely remember feeling safe the second I reached him in the woods, wishing that everything that had happened was all just a dream.

A glass of water sits on his desk across the room, and I see four sleeping bags laid out across the floor, one for each of my friends.

I take the covers off my legs and place my feet on the ground, the moment I put pressure on my leg I wince in pain. I try taking a few steps forward, but there is no use, I fall straight to the ground. I hear footsteps, running up the stairs.

Before I could even stand up, Sadie and Alec were in the room helping me back onto the bed.

"Hey?" her voice is soft, "What do you need? I can grab something for you if you want?"

I point to the water on the desk. Alec grabs the drink and sets it in my hands. As I take a few gulps, Sadie rubs the lower part of my back, making me feel twenty times better.

I can't help noticing the fact that Sadie and Alec and mouthing words to each other.

"You guys aren't telling me something." I catch them both off guard.

"Do you remember anything that happened?"

"Um, it's a little foggy," I turn to Alec now, "but I remember finding you in the forest, and feeling safe."

"Anything else?" He asks.

"I remember my leg hurting a lot, and not knowing who was following me." The look that they are giving me, makes me realize what they are asking. They want to know if I remember Spencer dying in my arms. As tears roll down my cheeks, Sadie wipes them away.

"Kayleigh, before you collapsed into my arms, you were frantic about the fact that Spencer was dead." Alec takes another deep breath and continues, "When you told us that, Reed and I went back the way you came to find him."

"Is he here?" Alec doesn't say anything, he only looks at Sadie. "Sadie? Is Spencer here?"

"Kayleigh, when Alec and Reed went back, there wasn't anyone there. There was no blood, no body, nothing."

"What? That can't be right. He took his last breath in my arms, and I felt him die."

"We believe you, one hundred percent, but we looked everywhere and couldn't find him."

They keep talking but nothing registers in my head. *How is it possible that Spencer wasn't there? Did they take his body? Does that mean he is back in the Bunker?* My heart hurts the more I think of what could have happened to him.

"I have to go back." My voice is frail, and barely over a whisper.

"What do you mean go back?" asks Sadie.

"I have to go back and get Spencer."

"Kayleigh, he wasn't there."

"I get that, but if he wasn't there then he is back in the Bunker."

"You can't be serious; how do you think you're going to get back into the Bunker?"

"You guys found me yesterday. I can't leave him there, whether he is dead or alive."

Once again Sadie and Alec communicate between themselves, but this time I feel more agitated. "Can someone please loop me in, why do you keep looking at each other like that?"

"Kayls, we didn't find you yesterday."

"What do you mean?"

"You've been out for the last week."

"A week?"

"You had lost a lot of blood by the time you reached us. We did everything we could to stop the bleeding, but nothing was working."

Sadie chimes in, "We were going to try and bring you to your place, but there were cops all over. Our best chance at keeping you alive was to bring you back to Alec and Kate's house. We were lucky their mom had just gotten home from the hospital. She was able to isolate the bleeding, but you weren't waking up."

"My mom said that hopefully within a few days, you'd wake up on your own."

"The four of us have been watching over you for the last week."

"I've been in a coma for a week?" They both nod their heads. "This can't be happening. Who knows what they could have done in the Bunker in a week? I have to go; I can't waste any more time."

"Kayleigh you can barely stand on your leg, how are you going to do this?"

"I don't know but I can't sit here and do nothing. You guys have no idea what it is they do down there, and if I can do something to help the people stuck there, then I have to."

"I can't lose my best friend again. I have been a wreck for the past week, I didn't know whether you were going to wake up, and now I might lose you again?" Sadie has tears dripping down her face, I grab a hold of her hands and look her in the eyes.

"You won't lose me again, I promise."

She wipes the tears with the back of her hand, "There is only one way that you can keep that promise." A look of confusion crosses my face, Sadie stands up and walks over to Alec, she whispers something into his ear and nods his head.

He grabs his phone and quickly types something in. Seconds later he receives a response, "They say they're in."

"They're in?" He nods, "In what?"

"The only way we won't lose you Kayls is if we go back with you."

"I can't let you guys come with me, it's too dangerous."

"We know. We have been talking about it for the last week, and we had a feeling you were going to want to go back."

"The four of us agreed that if you decide that you want to go back, there was no way we were letting you go alone."

"You guys are crazy."

They look at each other and then at me and smile, "We know."

ACKNOWLEDGEMENTS

I have been thinking about making this book a reality for a very long time, and I finally was able to put this idea into words, which I am so proud of.

None of this would have been possible without the support I got from my family and friends. To my mom and dad, for listening to me bounce ideas off the wall, and to my brother Louis, for not holding back on his ideas to make my book better. Thank you.

To my friends, Hannah, and Sofia, who took on the role of designing the cover on this book. I know I didn't make it easy for you two, but I am beyond grateful for what you created.

To everyone who read this book repeatedly, until it was just right.

To Kayleigh and Spencer, I spent so much time diving into your characters that I feel like you could be real people in my life. It makes me so happy that I was able to bring your characters to life.

Words could not describe how grateful I am for every one of you. Thank you.

ABOUT THE AUTHOR

ELIZABETH PTACK is a Canadian author, with a love for romance, fantasy, and sports, who dreamt of bringing her visions to life.

At an early age, Elizabeth imagined herself, creating a new world filled with dynamic characters and interesting stories.

Follow Elizabeth's journey:

Instagram:
@elizabethptack
@our.fated.love

Website:
Elizabethptack.com

Printed in Great Britain
by Amazon